CHARLY'S
EPICFIASCOS
Beware
of Boys

JE

Also by Kelli London

Charly's Epic Fiascos Series

Charly's Epic Fiascos

Reality Check

Star Power

Boyfriend Season Series

Boyfriend Season

Cali Boys

Uptown Dreams
The Break-Up Diaries, Vol. 1 (with Ni-Ni Simone)

Published by Kensington Publishing Corporation

CHARLY'S
EPICFIASCOS
Beware
of Boys

KELLI
LONDON

Dafina KTeen Books
KENSINGTON PUBLISHING CORP.
http://kensingtonbooks.com

DAFINA KTEEN BOOKS are published by

Kensington Publishing Corp.
119 West 40th Street
New York, NY 10018

All Kensington titles, imprints, and distributed lines are available at special quantity discounts for bulk purchases for sales promotion, premiums, fund-raising, and educational or institutional use.

Special book excerpts or customized printings can also be created to fit specific needs. For details, write or phone the office of the Kensington Special Sales Manager: Kensington Publishing Corp., 119 West 40th Street, New York, NY 10018. Attn. Special Sales Department. Phone: 1-800-221-2647.

KTeen logo Reg. U.S. Pat. & TM Off.
Sunburst logo Reg. U.S. Pat. & TM Off.

ISBN-13: 978-0-7582-8701-4
ISBN-10: 0-7582-8701-1
First Printing: February 2014

eISBN-13: 978-0-7582-8702-1
eISBN-10: 0-7582-8702-X
First Electronic Edition: February 2014

10 9 8 7 6 5 4 3

Printed in the United States of America

For T & C2 & K:
I lead; you follow. You lead; I follow.
Remember:
Actions, not words
Knowledge, not belief
Truth, not axiom
Sovereignty, not majority rule
Individuality, not popularity
Your story, not *History*

Love is classified as a noun, yet it's an action. Therefore live it and breathe it as a verb. You are mind—your thoughts manifest—therefore think, act, and become.
Loving you . . .

Acknowledgments

Family and loved ones: Your support and understanding my disappearing to write is greatly appreciated. I am fortunate to have you all in my life.

Fellow writers: Your dedication to writing is admired.

Selena James: Your dedication to the craft is admirable and inspirational.

R.M. Johnson and Dashawn Taylor: Thank you for the shoptalk and author powwows.

For my readers: Thank you for being you. Thanks for the emails, the support, and your dedication to following my works. You are truly, truly appreciated!

A note from Kelli

A wise person once wrote, "To whom much is given, much is required." In short, if you receive a lot, you should give just as much. Now while I'd love to take credit for the above quote, I can't. However, I do acknowledge that I am huge advocate of giving back. I hope that, if not now, one day you too will promote the same, as it's this merry-go-round of giving and receiving that makes the world a better place, and people, in general, happier. It—giving—is also something that all of us are capable of. If you don't believe me, just think about it. Consider how much you've been given, and I'm not talking about just tangible things. I'm not referring to hot shoes, funkier handbags, high-priced two-hundred-dollar jeans that are cut from the *same* denim as the ten-dollar jeans your local supersaver store carries, but are pricier because of the brand on them (ahh . . . bet you didn't know that, did you? ☺), or designer's names and labels we have to practice to pronounce. I'm speaking of good friends who listen, great educators who teach, the unconditional love our pets give us, the care and dedication of parents—all the things we sometimes overlook because we've lived with them and, unfortunately, sometimes have come to expect these things of them and don't give them much deserved appreciation, not the way we should. And just as we should appreciate, we should also reciprocate. Put that—giving back—on the top of your to-do list. Be a good friend. Help a stranger. Lend a hand to your elders. Read to a child. Do everything within your power to propel the world in a good way. You'll not only feel better for it, your life will be richer. Don't believe me? Well, turn the page. Charly can show you how.

Enjoy *Beware of Boys*, and feel free to borrow from Charly's fuel to help.

Stay strong. Stay beautiful. Stay you.

—Kelli

BOYS

V

~~Girls~~ Ain't Nothing But Trouble

—song by DJ Jazzy Jeff and The Fresh Prince (aka Will Smith)

remixed title: Charly St. James

note to self: Yes, boys can be trouble, but only if you allow them to be.

Prologue

Charly was in a storm of complete madness. Her purse was clutched to her side, a shopping bag was in one hand, and her cell was in the other. Her eyes widened, glued to the phone's screen. She was reeled in by the title of the online article that Lola, her best friend since forever, had urged her to read, but Lola kept interrupting Charly before she could. And Lola had interrupted everything else too, like Charly's relaxation and her efforts to focus on the pilot she was putting together. She was hoping the network would give her a new spin-off show that would make people over from the inside out. But it was what it was, and Lola, although a handful, had done Charly a favor by coming to New York to visit her while she took extra vacation time between tapings to accomplish her mission. She was also going to take Charly's dog, Marlow, back with her to Illinois while Charly went back on the road with the show.

Charly exhaled.

Yes, she was happy to have her best friend there, she reminded herself. She just wished Lola weren't so mesmerized by the big city. Lola elbowed her. "Give me a second, Lola," Charly said, trying to ignore the disruption of Lola and the shoppers, zeroing in on the headline again.

INSIDE ENTERTAINMENT: NEW YORK
INDUSTRY BAD BOYS UNITE TO HELP
GIRLS AT RISK

Lola elbowed Charly again, clearly having not heard Charly or not caring that Charly wanted to read the article, even though she'd been the one to insist that she did. Charly closed the Internet connection, deciding she'd read it later. "You know, you could've at least let me see who teamed up and what their plan is. You never know, it could be info that would help me with my spinoff," she snapped, irritated. She side-eyed Lola, and shook her head. Lola stood next to her with her mouth wide open, obviously amazed by something, but Charly didn't know what this time.

"Charly! Do you see all the shoes?" Lola asked, pushing her way through the crowded sneaker store, and making her way to the display case. "You know if you can get the new show, you can fit some of the girls in these. These are hot!"

Charly's eyebrows moved north. She didn't see what the big deal was. Yes, there were tons of sneakers, but what else would one expect in a store that specialized in all sorts of athletic shoes. And the last thing she'd planned to do once she got the new show was put girls in sneakers. "I see them. And stop saying my name, Lola! Didn't we just talk about that in the last three stores?" Charly asked, adjusting the sunglasses on her face. They'd been shopping for hours, and for just as long she hadn't been comfortable. What was supposed to have been sister-friends' day out to find Lola an outfit for to-morrow night's concert had turned into frenzy when Charly had been approached by fans of the show who'd refused to let her shop in peace. It wasn't that she'd minded the attention. She just didn't like when it became overwhelming, and it was way past that. She was just Charly, a girl from the Midwest who had fulfilled her dreams. But no one saw her that way anymore. That was what she'd been told for the past couple of seasons, but she hadn't believed it. She shook her head. The one thing she'd once desired—fame—was now coming back to teach her to be careful what she asked from the universe.

"Charly! Charly! Get over here," Lola shouted, clearly not caring about their discussion or Charly's discomfort. "Stop it already, you know you like the attention," Lola accused. " 'Least I know I do. Because of you, I keep get-ting discounts." Lola was smiling and holding up a pair of sneakers. "These are some hot tennis shoes, huh?" She sneezed, then wiggled her nose. "I hate these allergies," she said more loudly than necessary.

Charly gritted her teeth. She loved Lola like a sister, but she promised herself that after this trip, she wouldn't go shopping with Lola anymore. She heard Lola sneeze loudly again, then made a mental note to herself. Not only would she not shop with Lola anymore, she also wouldn't sleep anywhere near her again. The night before, Lola had positioned the guest trundle bed next to Charly's, and had kept sneezing in Charly's direction. Charly was sure she'd felt a spray or two.

"Here I come," she said, then tried to excuse herself through a small group of teens that had gathered between she and Lola, pretending she didn't see how they were looking at her. Some just gawked as if she were a circus attraction. Others were on their cell phones telling whomever they were talking to that Charly from television was standing feet from them. One or two were either snapping pictures or videoing her. "Sorry," she said, stepping on someone's foot. "Pardon me," she said to another. "So you're just not going to move? At all?" she snapped when one refused to budge, then locked eyes with Lola, who still stood in front of the display case with an *I'm sorry* look on her face that quickly turned into one of surprise.

"Oh. My. Yes! I so love New York!" Lola's voice shrilled as she screamed like she'd just won the lottery. "Charly! Charly!" she was saying with one sneaker in her hand, jumping up and down.

Charly didn't get a chance to answer her or see what all the fuss was about. "Huh?" she began.

A hand grabbed Charly's arm, pulling her through the crowd that had begun to thicken around her. "C'mon," a raspy male voice said, startling her.

"Let me go!" Charly said to whomever the hand belonged to, then tried to pry it from her arm, digging her nails into his smooth dark chocolate skin as her feet gave in to his strength, moving one in front of the other, no matter how hard she dug her heels into the ceramic floor to prevent herself from moving. "I said let me go!"

"Stop acting stupid. Can't you see I'm trying to help you?" he said in a tone raspier than before. Charly still couldn't see through the throng of teenagers. But she could hear him, and "stupid" didn't sit too well with her.

"Who are you calling stupid, Stupid?" she snapped, no longer needing his help to break free of the crowd that swarmed her. After whoever-he-was had insulted her, she'd pushed her way through, parting the teens and knocking some over like dominoes. She'd forgotten about etiquette and niceties and treating the fans special. But she hadn't forgotten about respect, and this dude had just disrespected her. "Aw, heck no. You must not know who I am, you lowlife. Get your nasty hand off me," she snapped after she'd pushed her way through the group, running face-first into someone's chest. Charly looked up, way up, ready to spit fire and throw hands, but she didn't. She was prepared for war, but she didn't want any casualties, and the person she'd run into would've definitely been an innocent victim, she decided. The hand that had pulled her through the crowd was still gripping her arm, and the person in front of her had both of his in his pockets, so it couldn't be him. Plus their complexions were different. One was smooth dark chocolate; the other was butter pecan. Finally, she successfully freed herself from whoever's death grip on her arm. "You idiot. You hard-up, stalking idiot," she yelled, then stopped when she saw that a fan was videoing them and heard the man in front of her clear his throat. She looked into his eyes.

The tall, butter-pecan guy met her with a smile. "Trust me, sweetheart, he didn't call you stupid. Why would he go out of his way for you if he thought you were stupid? He was saving you—just like he does all girls. And you may want to consider making nice for two reasons: one, because you should never bite the hand that feeds you, and two, because of that person over there." He pointed to a fan, who was obviously recording the whole scene. "They're going to sell that video or whatever to the tabloids or post it online, and it'll be viral in no time. And that's not good for you, especially since you're up for a new show." He winked, and Charly wondered how he knew.

"Oh. My." Lola sneezed. "God!" Lola was still shouting between sneezes. "Charly! Look. Look. You gotta look! He's one of them."

But Charly couldn't look if she'd wanted to. The red heat of rage was blurring her vision, and all she could think about was the fan uploading the video online, and the only thing she could see was the butter-pecan charmer who stood in front of her. His statement may have been warm, due to its being laced with *sweetheart*, and the smile he wore commanded ease. But he was much more than tall—he was massive. He looked as though he was close to seven feet and bench-pressed gyms, not weights, but his mind had to be small, she thought. She hadn't done anyone dirty who was responsible for her pay so, clearly, she hadn't bitten any hand that had fed her. One thing she didn't have to think about was his size. It prevented her from seeing the guy who stood behind him—the same guy who'd snatched her through the crowd, and now seemed to have one of his own swarming him. Charly crossed her arms, then nodded her head in the direction of her assailant. "Well, while he's at it, he may want to save himself too. He needs more help than I did," she spewed.

Butter Pecan turned around and transformed into an action hero. His chiseled arms moved left and right. In one swift motion he pushed down whoever, covered the other guy with what appeared to be a blanket, and then parted the crowd, pushing some away.

"Back up! I said, back up!" His calming voice changed into an authoritative, deep you-don't-want-none-of-this tone as he finished securing the area. His hand was on his ear pressing something; then he spoke into a miniscule microphone Charly couldn't see. It reminded her of the earplugs Secret Service for the White House were equipped with. "I need three inside the store and the trucks waiting. Alert store security that we'll need private exit escorts. He's right here. He's with me, so, of course, he's all clear."

"See. I told you to look!" Lola was still yelling. "Wish I was over there. I'd touch him too. Touch him for me, Charly! Touch him! At least get his autograph." Then Lola screamed again, this time louder. "Oh my God. There's another one! Look, Charly! Look! Outside the store! Is that Faizon walking with the cops?"

Charly rolled her eyes. Lola's excitement about her assailant and Faizon, a mega Hollywood actor who was nowhere outside of the sneaker store when she glanced out, was getting under her skin, and her level of anger was growing. She hadn't wanted to go shopping, and had begged Lola to stop yelling her name. Lola and her big mouth had incited all this mess, she tried to tell herself, then thought better of it. It wasn't Lola's fault. Charly could've left after her first fan frenzy. "You come touch him yourself, Lola. You couldn't pay me to touch him," she began. Then her jaw dropped when Butter Pecan stepped to the side to go meet three other massive men who'd rushed into the store with uniformed security. "Oh."

"You know, I grew up fighting bullies who thought I was soft because I wasn't in the streets, and I've toured the world a few times, and I've never, never, met anyone in my life as rude and disrespectful—as ungrateful—as you. Now I wish I could take it all back," Mēkel, the hottest, most gorgeous singer in the universe, said, staring into her eyes. He shook his head in disgust; then his lips pressed together, making his trademark pool-deep left dimple indent. His skin was the prettiest shade of chocolate she'd ever seen, and, upon closer inspection, she noticed he had a spatter of cute freckles across the bridge of his nose. "My moms raised us as a single mother after my father died, and she brought me up to believe that all females were queens. I wonder if she would've taught me that if she knew you."

"But—" Charly began, not knowing what to say. She wanted to defend herself but couldn't. In less than a second, Mēkel was whisked away by security.

"That was cool," Lola said, gripping two shopping bags filled with four pair of tennis shoes and zooming toward the exit doors. "Right, Charly?"

Charly kept pace with her physically, but mentally lagged behind. No, it wasn't cool to her. She had been surrounded and had clashed with one of her used-to-be-favorite singers, and she knew that the whole shebang would be on the Internet before she'd made it out of the mall. She pushed through the exit door onto the street, then gave Lola a side-eye. "No. It was—what in the . . . ?" she yelled, impacted by a sudden force. Her body jerked sideways, making her topple. She thrust out her arms to soften the fall, and caught sight of the force in her peripheral. A group of guys ran down the block, and one of them had her purse in his hands.

"Charly!" Lola yelled, simultaneously reaching out to help up her friend and scurrying toward the thieves at the same time. She moved one foot one way, then twelve inches back the other, clearly unable to decide between helping Charly or pursuing the perpetrators. "You okay? They snatched your purse?" she asked, looking down the block as Charly stood.

A motorcycle zoomed up, skidding to a stop in front of them. "You . . . ?" the rider said something, but Charly and Lola couldn't make it out. The voice was muffled behind the helmet.

Charly dusted off her knees and wiped the dirt and rocks from the palms of her hands. She looked at him, then pointed to her own head, hoping he understood she was referring to his helmet. "I can't hear you! Not with the helmet on."

The guy nodded, then slowly lifted the helmet's visor, revealing his chocolate complexion. Charly gulped. From what little she could see, the guy was scary looking. A thick scar was across his eye, and tattoos, like wallpaper, decorated the part of his neck that she could see. The scariest of all, though, were the three teardrops tatted under his eye. She had learned back in Chicago that teardrops were deadly trophy marks, each one standing for a life taken. "Here," the gruff voice said, then tossed her purse to her. "I think that's yours. Everything's there. They didn't have time. . . . I didn't give 'em time. Check it."

Charly looked at him, then down to her purse. She rifled through it, then nodded because she didn't know what else to do. She was confused. "I'm good."

He nodded, glaring at her through cold eyes. "You sure? Good, good. Like not-snitching good?"

Lola sucked her teeth.

Charly reared back her head, wincing. Snitch, though spelled with five letters, was equivalent to four-letter word where she came from. A curse. "I was always taught that snitches get stitches," she said, not knowing what she was going to do after this was over with. She was no fool though. Even if she planned on calling the cops, she'd never warn him. Not with the way he looked.

"True. True, good looking, and pardon those knuckleheads. They don't know no better, but they will. I'ma see to it. Trust!" he growled, flipped his visor back down, then sped off.

Charly stood watching him with wide eyes as he disappeared around the corner. For the life of her, she couldn't process what had just happened. Not at the rate it went. Two minutes ago, her purse had been snatched. Thirty seconds later, it had been returned.

"Check it!" Lola urged, walking up next to her. "Is everything in there?"

Charly snapped to, then opened her purse and rifled through it again. She nodded. It was all there, including her phone. She exhaled, not realizing she'd been holding her breath. "Nothing's missing." She looked at Lola, trying to read her expression, hoping that they felt the same way. Lola nodded as if she could read Charly's mind. "If we say anything—if this gets out—you know I won't be able to go to the concert. It's bad enough I'll probably be on the Internet later."

Lola laughed. "You're probably on there now! You and Mēkel, and I know he won't be happy about that, especially since he's known for helping girls."

Charly reared back her head, remembering the guy in the store had said something similar. "What do you mean?"

"Duh!" Lola said. "I asked you to read the article. Didn't you? Mēkel is one of the three who's formed the foundation to help girls." She shrugged, switching topics. "But what's important now is we'll be able to go to the concert. You got your purse back, and everything's in it. It makes no sense to cry about a mess after it's been cleaned up."

"Especially if crying will stop you from seeing RiRi perform!" Charly agreed, then walked forward and put her arm in the air. They needed a cab.

1

Charly's feet couldn't move her fast enough as she crushed down the aisle, surrounded by men who resembled huge trees, while she watched Lola leading the crew and pushing people out of the way. The lights were dimming, the audience was screaming, and teenagers, most wearing too much perfume or makeup, or not enough clothes, were scattered everywhere except in front of their purchased seats. Charly cringed as she made her way closer to the first row, shaking her head at Lola, who was in front of her, but only by a few feet and with a few different people sandwiched between them. Her breath caught in her throat as anxious adrenaline built inside her. She was sure that at any moment, her evening plans would change. She'd gotten dressed to have a good time, not fight, but she knew that before the night was over and after security stopped escorting her, she'd be mixed

up in a brawl-till-you-fall moment. Lola, who was proving herself a fan to the nth degree, had turned into a
human bulldozer, shoving concertgoers, one by one, to
clear the path.

"C'mon, Charly!" Lola urged, wiping her nose with
Kleenex and standing on the side of the front row. She
was waving her hand frantically, as if Charly were clear
across the auditorium instead of feet behind.

Charly held a finger to her lips, shushing Lola. The last
thing she needed—or wanted—was more attention, and
Lola knew it. After the blowup in the sneaker store, how
could Lola not get it, she wondered, then corrected her
thoughts. It wasn't like she was some huge celebrity,
that's what Charly kept telling herself. But she had to
admit that even though she considered herself just another teen, she wasn't. Not anymore. She and Lola had
been stopped three times in Madison Square Garden's
lobby by fans who'd wanted to take pictures with her
and get her autograph before she entered the arena.
Hired security, dressed in NYC cop blues, complete with
badges, had offered her an escort, then warned her that
she could prove to be a security risk if fans kept swarming her when she'd refused. But Charly didn't listen to the
police or the voice inside herself that told her that although she thought she was her old self, she wasn't. Instead, she'd opted for another pair of shades, and tried to
elude crowds by turning her head the other way. This
hadn't worked, and five-oh had ended up assigning a
staff team to take her to her seat. Now here she was,
flanked by giants who were outfitted in black shirts that
had the word STAFF stretched across their bodybuilder

physiques, and a senior citizen who was armed with a flashlight.

The senior citizen pushed past Charly and the staff, making his way to the front row. He looked at Lola, then shook his head, clearly irritated that she was acting like the Garden had hired her to get the crowd in check. He stepped around Lola as if she weren't there, and reached out his hand to a group who stood in front of the seats. "Tickets, please? Pass me your tickets so I can make sure you're supposed to be sitting here," he demanded, clicking on the flashlight like it was already dark in the arena, then shined the beam on their ticket stubs after they'd passed them to him.

"Well?" the staff guy up front asked the man with the tickets.

The senior citizen nodded. "They're clear, but . . ." He scratched his head. "We're going to have to relocate them for all the seats you need. The rest of the row's full."

Even over all the noise, Charly could hear the group protest, and she couldn't blame them. She wished someone would tell her she had to relocate after she'd bought her tickets and outfit. "That's not necessary," she yelled to the front, then tapped one of the security men on the shoulder, and repeated herself. "They bought their tickets just like I did. Why should they have to move?" she asked.

Staff guy gave her a side eye, clearly not caring about what she thought. "Because we say they do. Security measure," he explained after she looked at him like he was cuckoo. "You should've alerted the Garden that you were coming. Then we could've been prepared." He turned away from her, then nodded to one of the other tree-trunk-looking men wearing a STAFF shirt, standing up front.

The man returned the nod, then turned on the group in the first row. "Move down. We need four seats," he boomed.

"Yeah. Four seats," Lola parroted, bopping up and down in the two-hundred-dollar sneakers Charly had begged her not to buy because they were too close in color to her nutmeg complexion, making her look barefoot. They also didn't look good with her naturally platinum-blond hair and made her look fluorescent in the yellow outfit she wore.

"Four seats for what? There are only two of us," Charly began, then was interrupted by a crackling static sound coming simultaneously from all the staff's walkie-talkies.

The man in front of her grabbed the sides of his radio, then held it to his ear, listening intently. He moved it to his mouth, pressed a button, then mumbled something unintelligible to Charly's ears. Seconds later, another man dressed in similar shirt crossed the stage, making his way to them. He was just as huge as the rest, but, unlike the others, he wore a pleasant smile. "*Extreme Dream Team* Charly St. James, right?" he asked, marrying the show and her name together as if that were how her birth certificate read. He was towering feet above them, but his infectious smile made him seem closer.

Charly looked up and nodded. She returned his smile. "Yes. I'm Charly St. James—from *The Extreme Dream Team*."

"Yes!" Lola yelled, jumping up and down. "That's her. She's Charly."

He squatted down, then waved his hand for his fellow staff brethren to escort her to him. He held out his hand, then shook hers. "You should've had your people contact our people—then you could've entered through the private entrance. How many pluses do you have?"

Charly's eyebrows crinkled. "Pluses? Like math pluses and minuses?"

He laughed, then shook his head. "Sorry, I've been in the industry too long, so I tend to speak industry lingo. Pluses? Yes, like plus-ones on guest lists. Like Charly plus-one, or Charly plus-two. You've heard of that? How many people do you have with you?"

Now it was Charly's turn to laugh. If she and Lola had gotten into the Garden free, then she could claim to have a plus-one, but since they'd paid, there wasn't a freebie attached and she couldn't consider it anything other than paid for. "I bought our tickets, but there are two of us, if that's what you want to know."

He waved his hand as if disgusted. "Paid?" He raised his brows and pressed his lips together as if in thought, then relaxed. "Okay. Bring them up. Charly and her plus-one," he said to security. "Charly, you don't mind do you? RiRi invited you backstage, but if you'd prefer to watch from the front row, that's cool too. You can just meet after the concert. Seems she's a fan of your show."

Lola screamed, then ran toward the side of the stage with her hands waving in the air like she had been chosen to compete on *American Idol*. "I'm the plus-one. I'm the plus-one!" she yelled. "And I'm meeting RiRi."

Charly thanked the security guy, then followed the entourage of the tree-trunk-looking men who flanked her backstage. A slight smile parted her lips. To herself, she may have been just another girl, but she knew she had to digest that many didn't see her that way anymore. And that was all right with her, at least for tonight. Being invited backstage by the princess of R & B/hip-hop was a perk she could learn to live with it.

"Hurry, Charly!" Lola urged, waiting for Charly. More security was protecting the stairs that led to the stage, and they wouldn't let Lola up.

Charly strutted, getting there as quickly as she could. She was barely five feet behind Lola, but it felt like more than fifty feet separated them. Finally, she made it. "All right, all right already," she said, then turned to the giants clad in STAFF shirts. "Thank you. Next time I'll have my people contact your people," she said to them, then locked arms with Lola and climbed the stairs. "And start acting your age, Lola. You're seventeen and acting elementary. It's embarrassing."

The view from stage left was more amazing than Charly would've ever imagined. She took in the lights, production, music, and background dancers, and gained more appreciation for the work behind the concert scene, which, to her, wasn't too different from the hard labor that she and the crew of *The Extreme Dream Team* put into their show. After they'd put in all the work, the show was presented in a neat package, but the audience would never know what went into creating the gift. And Charly was sure that RiRi labored just as hard because every-

thing seemed effortless, which was a sign of diligent practice.

"You see her?" Lola asked, sniffling and pointing to
RiRi, the songstress from the islands. She was stunning,
and she sounded as good in person as she did on her
tracks. "She just pointed and waved at you," Lola said,
acting like the true fan she was, while reaching into her
small purse and taking out an allergy pill, which she
popped into her mouth and swallowed dry.

Charly elbowed Lola, then waved back. She grinned so
hard her cheeks hurt. "Yes. Yes, I see her. But wait . . . do
you see her head? Her hair's messed up." Charly jumped
up and down, frantically waving her hands in the air to
get RiRi's attention. When RiRi looked at her, Charly
pointed to her own hair, acting as if she were flattening it,
then swooping it behind her ear. She thrust her index finger toward RiRi, mouthing, *You. Fix it!*

RiRi pointed to her chest, still singing, then nodded
when Charly confirmed she was talking to her. RiRi did
as she was told, but still had hair standing up on her head
as if she had a jolt of static pulling it up from above. She
held up her thumb to Charly, asking if she'd accom-
plished fixing her do.

"Oh. God. Don't turn around. It's him." Lola said,
reaching over and giving Charly's wrist a death grip.

The blood stopped flowing to Charly's hand. "Lola, let
go." She shook her head in the negative at RiRi, while
trying to wriggle free of Lola's grasp.

"Behind you," Lola unsuccessfully tried to whisper.

Just as Charly was about to turn her head, she heard

RiRi say her name. RiRi waved her out, then exited off the other side of the stage, excusing herself with one finger held in the air, and nodding toward her main backup singer, who introduced Charly. "Everybody, give it up for Charly from *The Extreme Dream Team*! Guess she's not too happy with RiRi's hair. I guess that's why she's getting her own extreme makeover show, huh?" The audience cheered, and Charly's heart hit her knees as she wondered how everyone knew of her plans. Plans that weren't guaranteed by contract. "C'mon on out, Charly! And you too, the other surprise—bring Charly out with you," the backup singer said, waving.

The audience cheered, and a shoulder brushed against her, but Charly couldn't have seen whomever it belonged to if she wanted. It was just that dark on the side of the stage. "Beg your pardon," a male voice said in a familiar raspy tone, one that was delicious and not mean like Mēkel's had been in the store. A voice Charly was sure belonged to RiRi's other surprise.

Whoever it was moved in front of her now, and grabbed her hand, pulling her on stage as RiRi reappeared from the other side with a mirror in her hand. In the breeze of time, Charly's heart stopped. Whoever wasn't just Whoever anymore, and the delicious raspy voice was no longer delicious. Mēkel. They were literally inches from one another. He smiled as if they were old friends; then the light in his eyes died as he penetrated her with the softest baby-browns she'd ever encountered. She knew he would have frozen them to a dull-brown if he could. As if he hadn't just hit her with a piercing glance, Mēkel took a step toward her, wrapped his arm around her, and waved to the audience, whispering between teeth clenched in a phony smile, "This isn't for you. It's a charade for the fans and RiRi. If you can be professional enough, do us all a favor and play along."

Charly gritted her teeth, mimicked Mēkel's show for the fans, and then walked away, making her way toward the headliner. She was still waving out to the audience, but Charly couldn't see anyone. The lights were too bright and her heart was racing too fast for her to have full sight and comprehension. She was excited to be on stage, yet deathly afraid of it. But she didn't know the word for what she'd become, and didn't know if one existed to explain. All she knew was that she was a bundle of nerves, overwhelmed to be in front of the sold-out arena. She was used to working a small show, not standing and waving and smiling to thousands of people. She inhaled, snuck a look at Mēkel, and wanted to kick herself. She couldn't stand him, and could feel the contempt he had for her, but she was also melting because he was so gorgeous, standing there and running one of his hands over his semi-wild hair. He pushed his natural waves back, preventing them from falling in his face, and for a second she wished they hadn't clashed the day before, so she could touch it.

"Say something to the people, Charly," Mēkel said as a stagehand handed Charly a cordless microphone.

Charly took the microphone in one hand, and reached out and fixed RiRi's hair with the other while RiRi held up the mirror, smiling as Charly worked her magic. "A diva like this has to always look like the diva she is, wouldn't you all agree?" Charly said to the crowd of thousands of concertgoers, smiling. "Now enjoy the con-cert, because I will." She handed the microphone back to the stagehand who had brought it to her. She waved both palms toward the audience, then blew kisses before a thought hit her. She grabbed the mic again. "And don't forget to watch *The Extreme Dream Team*!" she added, then strutted off stage. She may've been there to attend the concert, but it was always time to work.

2

Th-thump. Th-thump.

No way! Really? Charly thought, trying to calm her anxious heart, which was beating heavier by the second. She furrowed her brows in wonder while scanning the room, looking for any sign of a joke being played on her, but found none. It was hard for her to believe that she'd been specially requested by three huge celebrities to help on a project that would benefit girls in Las Vegas—a request she wasn't supposed to know about yet. It was even more baffling that they'd stipulated that none of their names would be revealed until after she'd agreed. Their request: that she wanted the project because of its significance, not their celebrity, at least that what Liam had whispered to her in confidence when she'd stepped in the room. He'd walked in minutes before her, and, obviously had overheard more than he was supposed to. She scanned the paper in her hand for the umpteenth time in less than five minutes, and was totally in. The project would be a joint venture to build and design a structure to help girls who had beat a deadly disease or were fighting to do so. She nodded. Of course she'd do it, just like she'd told Mr. Day, the show's executive, who'd taken on a father-figure role with her, right before she'd slipped, telling him she knew about the celebrities involvement. She looked up and held her hand to her chest, then clenched her teeth in an attempt to prevent facial expression. She hoped the internal shock she felt hadn't surfaced.

The *really?* she had been mentally asking was really and truly really apparent, judging by the head nod she was receiving from one of the Suits in Boots, the nickname she had for Mr. Day's executively dressed assistants. Now, though, she was heavily weighing the possibility of changing this one's name to Bobble Head because he was bouncing his dome like one of the toys mounted on a car dashboard.

Th-thump-th-thump-th-thump. Now her heartbeat kicked up a gear, banging loudly in her ears, and she was sure that someone else in the room had to hear the drumming too. She gulped, almost frozen in disbelief. Blinking slowly, she couldn't understand why everyone else was smiling when the world had just stopped spinning.

"Oh, and I forgot to mention that we need to talk later," Mr. Day was saying, pointing to his desk. "It seems you've gone viral, and not in a good way. You need to go over to the publicist after we're done here to learn how to clean up the Mēkel mess, and figure out how to address all these rumors of you having an *Extreme Fashion* show or whatever they're calling it. All press isn't good press, Charly," he chastised.

Charly nodded.

"I'm serious, Charly," Mr. Day continued. "And from the call I received earlier today, the blowup you and Mēkel had in the store almost killed this opportunity. News spreads fast in entertainment, and no one wants to work with someone who has altercations—and they don't want to give them their own shows. Got it?"

Charly nodded again. She knew Mr. Day was right, but it was hard for her to think about anything else but the project at hand, and finding out who was behind it, something Liam couldn't tell her because even he didn't know. "So, they really asked for me? An athlete, actor, and an artist . . . as in what kind of artist? Artist is too general." She was deviating from Mr. Day's point, prying, but the not knowing was killing her, especially since she'd just agreed to take it on.

"Yes, they did. Big news. Right, love?" Liam, her co-host and pseudo boyfriend, asked with a smile in his voice, walking up behind her and massaging her shoulders.

Charly nodded like Bobble Head. Yes, the news was big. Huge. It was too enormous for her to take it all in without panicking. She pointed to her chest, questioning again, and wiggled her nose, which had begun to itch. Liam playfully pushed away her finger from her shirt. "Cachoo," she sneezed into the bend of her elbow. "Sorry." She collected herself. "Can't you just tell me now? I mean you know I'm in, so what's the big deal. Why do I have to wait?" She crossed her arms.

Mr. Day laughed, putting one hand in his pocket and wagging his index at her with the other, while giving Liam a disappointed look for telling. "Call it your punishment for not knowing how to behave in public," he stated, looking back at Charly. "And to your first question, yes, Charly. *You.* They specifically asked for you, and didn't present the offer to anyone else. And they want to talk to you too. All of them but one, in particular, is adamant. It's time you met the team," he said. "First, though, let me warn you that their attorney thought you knew about this a week ago. I knew you wouldn't turn it down—not that you could've anyway, according to your contract. But they don't know that. So I told everyone last week that you were definitely in and excited." He shrugged, then waved her closer. "I lied to the network—to everyone, in fact—to cover your behind while you extended your vacation by a couple days, and took it upon yourself not to answer my calls. If you had've, you would've been informed of this before now."

"But I needed the break, Mr. Day. I didn't purposely avoid your calls; I left my phone in another room at home, so I could relax," she lied. "We've been working nonstop for forever," she explained, walking over and joining him next to the desk.

"I know, that's why I lied. But it's not a big deal. The network and the attorney who's representing the joint venture were the only ones in talks, putting this together. So just go along with it. Now, for the big reveal." He winked, then spun the speakerphone around on the desk and pressed a button. "This is Day. Thanks for holding. Are you all there?" he asked, his face turned toward the intercom.

A male voice answered, "Yeah." Charly closed her eyes, hoping whoever it was would speak again so she could try to place him. He didn't sound familiar. In fact, he'd barely sounded at all; his answer had been so low and monotone. It piqued her curiosity. She didn't see the need for their hiding until she agreed. It wasn't like they were requesting her help to do something bad. Charly and *The Extreme Dream Team*'s job was helping people, not hurting them. She shrugged.

"Yeah, man, we're here," a familiar one, very distinctive said. Without hesitation or doubt, Charly knew whom the West Indian accent belonged to. Faizon, the Hollywood A-list actor that Lola had thought she had spotted. Charly knew his voice well, and had listened to his enunciation closely time and time again, booming out of theater speakers, but never before had his words moved her so. Not like now. She shook her head, mouthing his name to Mr. Day. Mr. Day nodded confirmation, and her heart dropped to her knees.

"Yes, Day. Golden Boy, here. We're all on," a third one, whose tone was just as captivating as Faizon's but much deeper, added. "Where's Charly? Is she there with you, Day? Charly? Baby, you there?" the guy asked in his baritone, addressing her as if they were old friends. Charly's lips spread into a wide smile. Golden Boy was Lex, the greatest boxer of his division and also one of the youngest in his profession to skyrocket to the one-round-knockout status of Mike Tyson. And like his predecessor, he'd been known to street fight, but had cleaned up.

Charly was about to answer him, but the tickle in her nostrils and the tingle in her throat stopped her. She opened her jaws, inhaling, and closed her eyes. Her shoulders bounced as another sneeze surfaced, and, not wanting the guys on the phone to hear, she closed her lips and held it in. Immediately, she regretted it as it ricocheted off the back of her throat. She felt as though someone had chopped her, then released the air in a small sputter. "I think I've developed allergies," she explained very low, remembering Lola hadn't always suffered seasonal allergies, but, somehow, they'd recently kicked in. Charly shook her head. She lived in a city that was almost devoid of greenery compared to the Midwest, where she hailed from, but anything was possible, including her being allergic.

Liam's hands tightened on Charly's shoulders, digging under her clavicle bone and into her muscle. She buckled slightly under his strong fingers, and shot him a look. He relaxed his hands. "Sorry, love. It was an accident," he explained with a small smile and raised brows.

"Yes. Yes. I'm here," Charly said with a smile in her answer. She was trying not to blush, but it was hard to keep the blood from rushing to her face after she'd received news of being requested by such big-time celebrities to help with such an important project. It was a mission that any girl on the planet would trade in her best pair of shoes and cash out her savings account to be a part of. "I'm so excited to find out about this."

"Wait, hold up! Word was you found out the science last week. You not saying you just found out, mama? Right?" Faizon questioned.

Charly shook her head at her mistake, then shrugged her apology to Mr. Day, who was staring her down. "No . . . I

knew, I just . . . I don't know. It's just so exciting to be able
to help with something this big," she lied, covering herself.
"Of course I knew. Mr. Day told me a week ago," she said,
parroting Mr. Day's words.

The quiet one spoke again. "So you knew about the
project *and* us—that we were behind it? You should've
known."

Charly looked at Mr. Day for help. He nodded. "Sure.
Of course. That was the terms, right. I agreed to take on
the project based on what it was, not who was behind it,
and then I found out you guys put it together." She nodded, mimicking Mr. Day, who stood across from her
moving his head up and down and smiling. "I love that
you guys wanted to make sure I was wooed by the project. That was smart."

Quiet guy laughed, low and sinister. "I told y'all she
knew."

Lex cut him off. "Good. Good. I'm glad you're just as
excited as we are. So I know you've already agreed, because if not we wouldn't be speaking. But I need to hear
you say it. So, are you in? Are you going to help us hook
up the girls in Vegas? Can you manage all of our requests: hip-hop, athletics, and theater?" he asked, his
voice seeming deeper. Charly smiled, finally figuring out
what type of art to incorporate into the project, and
thought she was going to go into cardiac arrest right
there on the spot. What else could she do when two of
the hottest and cutest male celebrities were on the line at
the same time, and they were calling especially for her?
She had no idea who the quiet one was, but she was sat-
isfied with the gorgeous duo, so it didn't matter if num-

ber three was fine or not. She was just happy to know that he was in hip-hop—that would help her try to figure out who he was.

"Yes, I'm in. How could I not be after reading the mission statement? I wish there had been a center like the one you're building when I was chasing my dream," she stated truthfully. "Not too many guys would come together for something this big. The fact that you all have been affected by a female in your lives fighting a deadly disease, and want to do something about it is phenomenal. Especially marrying all your professions—fitness, music, and theatre . . . incredible. Just incredible." She raised her brows, thinking how huge the project could be. How much girls like Lola and her sister, Stormy, could benefit from having a center to go to like the one the guys were building. "I just need to look at the requirements you listed once more to be sure I incorporate everything you guys need," she said. "Okay, Lex?"

"Ahh-haa," Lex's deep voice moaned through the intercom. "So Charly knows my voice? Y'all hear that? Especially you, Faizon. Huh, Fai? She knows *my* voice, and I don't act. I swing and knock out. No words needed for that," he teased.

"Nah, son. You cheated. You said Golden Boy. Everybody knows you're Golden Boy with the golden eyes," Faizon answered, laughing.

Liam cleared his throat. "Or perhaps, it's because of your showmanship—I mean sportsmanship, Lex," he suggested, referring to the trash talk Lex was known for inside of and outside the ring. "Her knowing who's behind the project could also be the reason. We did find out days ago, remember?" Liam threw in, nodding at Mr. Day and Charly.

Loud laughter blared through the intercom, and Mr. Day and his Suits in Boots joined in. Charly beamed, enjoying all the fuss over her and admiring Liam's courage. His comment proved that he wasn't intimidated by Lex's reputation of being the youngest one-round-TKO middleweight boxer.

"Peace. Peace. I gotcha, Liam," Lex said. "Protecting your territory, huh? I don't blame you. You s'posed to do that."

"Either that or he's marking it, nah'mean?" Faizon chimed in.

Charly's heart stopped. She didn't appreciate being objectified. She was a person—her own—not a thing, and especially not someone's territory. "All right, that's enough, guys." She rolled her eyes, but couldn't keep lightheartedness from her voice. "I know you all may be four of the hottest dudes to grace the earth," she said and averted her eyes to Liam, making sure he knew he was included. "But, hot or not, let me tell you none of you are *that* fantastic. Not enough to treat me less than my worth. Understand?" She scanned the room, spreading her glare around, then swallowed another sneeze, which made her body quake. All heads nodded, including those of Mr. Day and his assistants, who'd even chuckled beneath their breath. Charly heard a deep "yes, ma'am" come over the intercom, and knew it was Lex. "Understand?" she repeated, walking closer to the speakerphone. "I didn't hear the other apologies? Did you two hear me?" she questioned.

A warm chuckle preceded Faizon's half-cocked apology. "See, mama, this is why you got chose. Correction, this is why I knew you could collab with our project," Faizon began. "You're what we'd call a soldier in the streets—you down for yours, and take absolutely no mess, Charly. Straight up and down, mama, you're strong, beautiful, and a survivor. I researched you. I know who you are and what you bringing to the table. You're the perfect fit."

Charly crossed her arms and tapped the toe of her shoe against the carpeted floor. Faizon may've said something nice, but he was skirting her demand. "Apology, Faizon," she reminded.

Faizon laughed. "A'ight. A'ight. You got me, mama. I sincerely apologize. That's my word."

Charly cleared her throat. "Okay, that's two. I have the apologies of the athlete, the actor, and I'm sure my co-host will apologize. So what about yours, Mr. Music Industry?" Charly said, using his profession because she didn't know his name. Dead air filled the room.

"You know I'd never disrespect you, love," Liam said loudly, walking over to Charly. He planted a kiss on her cheek. He moved her long, curly hair from her face, then leaned in. "Not on purpose. Please accept my apology," he whispered in her ear.

Mr. Day broke up Charly's moment with Liam, thrusting manila folders at them. "Time to work," he said. "Liam, the top one's yours. It has a list of structure requests. Charly, the other is for you." He turned his attention back to the intercom. "All right, fellas, we thank you for the request, but we have to get going to get straight to work on our end. So unless there's anything else, we need to get started."

A few "nos" and "I'm goods" were heard before everyone bid their individual good-byes, and Charly promised them she'd be in touch before the lines disconnected.

Charly opened the folder Mr. Day had given her, and glanced at the few lines. She zeroed in on it, and the only thing she took in was addresses. "Where are the plans? The list of needs? What I saw earlier? This is just a sheet of paper, and it looks like a schedule," she said.

Mr. Day stepped closer, then reached out and tapped the sheet. "Three pieces of paper, Charly. But, as you can see, there are no plans, no mandatory requests. Not for you." He grabbed the folder, removed the first sheet, and ran the tip of his finger over the other. "Look here," he said, handing the folder back to her. "This is your itinerary. You and the guys will come up with your own plans for the center. They started with the landscaping and clubhouse or outside library or whatever it is they're taking charge on. They want you to take the lead on the project design for the girls' retreat . . . give some suggestions and make it pop. Believe me, they need it. They can't see past pink, purple—colors they think girls like—and their respective professions."

Liam took the folder from Charly before she could look at, showing himself to be more jealous than she had expected. "Itinerary? We're talking itinerary like plane and hotel arrangements?" He held up the folder as if he were farsighted. He shook his head no. "Not a good look, Mr. Day. Charly can't travel to meet them by herself. I have to go with her." He adjusted the printed itinerary.

Charly snatched the folder from Liam. First, he'd objectified her. Now he was acting like her father or guardian? "Calm it down, Liam. Insecurity isn't a good look for you," she said, referring to his obvious jealousy. "Besides, I've traveled for other shows to get a feel for them, for what they needed."

Liam crossed his arms and audibly huffed. "That's the problem, love. Seems they want to get a feel of something too. Especially that Lex character. I don't know what you did or when, but you must've really impressed him."

Charly elbowed him in the gut. "Watch your mouth."

Mr. Day gave them a knowing look and laughed. "If I didn't know any better, I'd say you two are really in a relationship, instead of just pretending to be in one for the cameras and television ratings." He eyed Liam. "But that's not the case. Right, Liam?" His question was more of a suggestion. "Liam, you'll be there in a few days to begin, but, Charly," he said, turning his attention to her, "you're leaving for Vegas tomorrow. That's not only where the project is, it's also where Lex's new training camp is, and right now he's training for his upcoming Showtime special, which will be taped in one of the casinos. So consider Lex the middle ground on this. The others have to meet there because Lex can't take a full day off due to the training. And let me warn you, you'll have to use your time wisely—get the plans together quickly. Faizon has an upcoming movie shoot in Hollywood, so he'll be in and out. And Mēkel's recording and practicing for his upcoming tour in Los Angeles, so the schedule is tight."

"*Mēkel?*" Charly said, her voice rising with panic and anger. "Did you just say Mēkel?" She stood, and looked down at the paper again, this time really reading it. She shook her head. His name was right there in black and white. "Wait a minute. I thought they—he, Mēkel, was working on a New York project with some other guys."

"Yes. I said Mēkel. Which is the reason we almost lost the project, but the contracts were already signed. I suggest you do whatever you can to fix it, because I heard he's looking for a loophole to get out. And as far as him working on a New York project . . . as I said before, Charly. Bad press. Bad press. The guys were meeting in New York to look at a couple of projects similar to theirs, not making a deal for a project in New York. The contracts had been signed and the ink was already dry for the Las Vegas retreat. Now you see what I mean about bad press," he said, chastising again, then got back to business. "Also, your chaperone's information is on there too. She's worked with Lex's people before, and checks out great. She's also the grandmotherly type who'll take care of you, so there are no worries." He shot Liam a look, like Liam was the one to approve Charly's affairs. "Okay?"

Liam nodded.

Charly shook her head. No, it wasn't okay. Nothing was cool with her and Mēkel.

Mr. Day pointed. "And you might want to check out that third sheet, Charly. That's the biggest news yet." He smiled and winked.

Charly flipped over the paper, and gulped. "Does this say what I think it says?"

Mr. Day nodded. "Yes, you can read. That's how huge this is, and that's how great I am—how much I believe in you and Liam. Once you complete this project and work on the others with the guys—they're opening multiple girls' retreats throughout the country—you'll get your other makeover show, which will air immediately following *The Extreme Dream Team*. You're only going to get a one-season contract, but it's a beginning."

3

Charly stood in the middle of the tarmac with one hand on her hip and the other drying her runny nose with the kazillionth Kleenex she'd used since she'd left New York. Drowsy from the allergy medicine she'd taken again just an hour before, her usually sharp brain was discombobulated, and she had a hard time comprehending what she didn't see at Las Vegas's airport. One, she thought, it should have been much bigger and, two, Vegas was a tourist spot, so surely the plane should've had a walkway that connected to the terminal. She looked at the small aircraft's stairwell, waiting for the other passengers to deplane. Passengers she'd never gotten a chance to see because she'd reached the airstrip around five-ish in the morning, right after she'd guzzled a dose of nighttime Benadryl. She had been the first one to board, and had immediately fallen asleep after she'd buckled in and cozied up with a blanket in the smallest first-class section she'd ever seen. It was now around seven in the morning, Pacific Standard Time, and her eyes were still heavy. She stretched, almost knocking off the large sunglasses that covered most of her face, then adjusted her floppy yet fashionable sun hat, which was pulled down over the tops of her ears. She may not have been a Rihanna or a Taylor, but she'd accumulated enough television time and fans to want to hide from the public when she wasn't looking her best. "Where is everybody?" she asked no one, seeing the flight attendants descend the staircase, which had wheels underneath it.

Charly turned toward the terminal where the flight attendants had instructed her to go before she'd departed the craft. An SUV pulled up behind her, pulling her attention as it zoomed, then screeched to a stop. She glanced at the large black vehicle, thinking it strange for an SUV to be on the runway, especially one that moved like it was from NASCAR. It had to be dangerous for anything with wheels, other than vehicles belonging to the airport, to be on the tarmac. She shrugged. So far everything about Las Vegas was a bit weird to her. Strange and desolate, she decided, looking around and getting a better view of her surroundings. She spotted only a few other planes and a handful of people walking around, most of them dressed in some sort of blah-colored airport gear.

"Excuse me? Charly St. James?" a woman's voice called from the direction of the black SUV.

Charly turned back toward the vehicle and eased her sunglasses down the bridge of her nose. The woman she'd set her eyes on was at least six-foot-two and dressed in a full business suit. Her hair was pulled back in a messy bun and she looked like a mannequin. She was also young looking, and not grandmotherly like Mr. Day had described her chaperone. Charly didn't know who she was, so she decided to be cautious. "Yes?" she answered, then hated that she did because immediately her head started to pound.

A big smile spread across the woman's face, and she began to walk over to Charly. "Ms. St. James, I'm Eden Gardens," she said, nearing Charly in seconds, thanks to her long elegant strut.

Charly nodded, then pursed her lips. She was trying to refrain from uttering the words whirling through her mind. *Garden of Eden.* "Oh . . . kay, and that means?" Charly said. She wasn't trying to be rude, but she didn't know the woman and she didn't want to ask too many questions, because then she'd have to keep thinking and responding. She'd better be quiet or else it was going to pound even more.

"That means I'm your chaperone." She smiled wider. "Didn't they tell you I'd be here for you, sis?"

Even though stretching her lips was a task because of being medicated, Charly returned the smile. This Eden Gardens may have been her chaperone, but she didn't exude authority. Her referring to Charly as sis made Charly feel they were on equal ground. She didn't feel like she had to be on guard or uneasy around her. Giving Eden the once-over, Charly appreciated the woman's style, even though she questioned how the woman wasn't sweating in the sweltering Las Vegas heat. Upon closer inspection, she found it hard to keep from calling her Garden of Eden because Eden, who'd looked like a mannequin when she was yards away, was almost a vision of perfection up close and her vibe was soothing. The woman had perfect skin, a build models would starve and beg for, and her smile radiated warmth and kindness. In a neat package, Eden exuded the confidence Charly wanted the girls on the show she was planning to have once she was finished making them over from the inside out. Eden also didn't look old enough to be anyone's chaperone. Charly wouldn't have guessed her to be over twenty-five, give or take a year. She shrugged, blaming it on Eden's beauty and melanin, and appreciated the comfort the woman's presence offered.

"It's truly nice to meet you. Please call me Charly," Charly said, nasally, suddenly feeling even more stuffed up.

Eden proffered her hand. "Only if you'll call me Eden, and try not to view me as your warden. I know a lot of celebs view us that way, because we're hired chaperones, and many think that means guardians. So, I just want you to know I'm here to get you where you have to go, make sure you're okay, and make sure you have everything and anything you need. But I'm not here to police you, just provide."

"I like you, Eden," Charly said, shaking Eden's hand. Now she really dug Eden's style, especially the no-policing part of it. "Okay, so I guess we just need to stop by baggage claim, so I can grab my luggage, then we're off." She removed her palm from Eden's, then blew her nose. "That is . . . if we're safe. You drove up like you were at a drag strip, not an airport, so I'm not so sure about that," she added as an afterthought.

"Whip—I mean the driver—used to . . . well, you're kind of right; he used to race, but you have nothing to worry about, he won't drive that way with you in the car." Eden laughed, then shook her head in wonder. "And carry your own bags? Really? Charly. Charly. Charly. You're fresh—new—unaffected. No diva tendencies. I like that! You're going to be a pleasure to work with. And I hope your cold gets better." She walked toward the limo.

Charly tilted her head, following Eden. She knew she wasn't like many assumed she'd be; she'd heard that many times. What hadn't graced her hearing was that she was a pleasure to work with. She was much too jazzy for the average person. She spoke her mind, and that usually didn't go over too well with others. "Just allergies. Unaffected? How?" she asked Eden.

"You're refreshing, Charly. How many people's egos wouldn't be affected by being flown out private? Seems you're pretty special." Eden winked, then rapped her knuckles against the vehicle, obviously trying to get the driver's attention. "And you have a great sense of humor too. You know there's no baggage claim here. Not at a private airport." She laughed and waved her hand at Charly's statement, obviously mistaking it as a joke.

Charly shrugged, then laughed at herself, though she hadn't meant to be funny. Flying private had been the furthest thing from her mind when she'd boarded and after she'd landed. Yes, she'd flown exclusive—that's what first class was to her—but she had been too tired to think about how she was traveling when she had gotten on the plane in Teterboro, New Jersey, which was nicknamed the Clearport. It was barely ten miles outside of New York, and served as the favorite airport of VIPs, or so Mr. Day had told her. Now she understood why she had only seen a couple other people getting off the plane. It wasn't a flight many could've afforded, and she put herself in that same category because she wouldn't buy anything too pricey—unless, of course, someone counted bags and shoes. "All right for my being refreshing and funny, Eden. Ready when you are," she said, but thought, *All right for me not knowing commercial from private. That's one I won't ever admit.* She laughed at her own joke, then cringed from her pounding temples. "Thank you," she said to Eden, who'd opened the back door for her, then slid inside the SUV.

"No problem," Eden said with a smile in her voice.

Charly could hear the driver adjusting her luggage in the trunk before he closed it, then heard him make his way to the side of the SUV, rapping a 2 Chainz song. The door banged shut, making the vehicle move. Charly jumped, opening her eyes, which she hadn't even realized she'd closed. Eden sat next to her, thumbing through a notebook, then turned her attention toward the front and deliberately cleared her throat.

"Don't forget," Eden said to the driver, biting her lip and wearing a concerned expression. "And you do remember the way, right?"

The driver half turned. "Whip won't whip the whip. That's what I promised, right? Professional. Got it. And of course I know where I'm going. Vegas belongs to me." He closed the divider that separated the front of the SUV from the back before Eden could respond.

Eden nodded, and her worried look disappeared. "Whip, his nickname," she said, shrugging her shoulders and shaking her head. "Lex had a different camp out here, and we just moved to the new location less than a week ago. That's why I asked Whip if he knew where he was going," she explained. She crossed her mile-long legs, then gave the notebook her undivided attention. Charly almost asked her what she was reading, but she didn't want to disturb her. She wanted to sleep. Eden looked at her, then nodded. "You might as well get some more rest while you can. It's going to be a long day, I'm sure." Eden half stood and reached forward, knocking on the divider. "Please *continue* to drive at a comfortable speed."

"Thank you," Charly said, glad for the reprieve. She needed a siesta, even if it was only for a few minutes. "Are we checking into my room—" She stopped, interrupted by the SUV suddenly racing at lightening speed.

Eden stomped her foot on the floor of the vehicle, shaking her head. The SUV slowed. She shook her head, then looked puzzled. "Room? Hotel room? Should I book you a room?" Her tone bordered on anxious.

Even though she was tired, Charly perked up. Surely the network wouldn't have let her travel to Las Vegas without accommodations. She pursed her lips. "I'm not being rude, but I have to stay somewhere, Eden. This isn't a one-day turn-around trip, you know?"

Eden smiled that warm smile again, and made Charly's tenseness almost disappear. "Of course you do. There's a private guest cottage on Lex's property where the training camp is, and it's all set up for you. They thought it would be better for you to work close together, proximity wise, that is. Plus, if you were up in one of the penthouse suites at one of the casinos, you'd all get rushed by fans and paparazzi—none of you would be able to work, especially with the leaks."

"Leaks?" Charly questioned.

Eden pressed her lips together. "Yes, leaks. Multiple ones. First the story leaked about the girls' retreat, and it was wrong, of course. Then we fixed it. And there was the leak about you hosting a show for the retreat before we went public. And now there's talk about you getting a show." Her smile returned, and Charly wondered how everyone knew she was pushing for another show. "See, you and the guys are hot topics."

"Wow. I haven't even signed papers yet, which means my show is in talks. As you know, nothing is concrete until the cement is poured, dried, and walked on." Charly nodded. That was all she could do because she was so tired. "And the cottage sounds good. Please wake me when we get close. I want to refresh my face before we get there," she said.

Eden laughed again, this time softer and lower. "Charly. Charly. Charly. No worries. Remember, you'll be staying in your own place. You'll have plenty of time to nap and freshen up before your meeting. And hopefully your medication will kick in before then." Eden flipped through some papers, then pulled one out of the pile. She handed it over to Charly. "I know you're tired, but I need to show you this. See. That's your itinerary for the week. Faizon isn't scheduled to be here until tomorrow morning, and who knows when or if Mēkel will show—he may just send his people to handle his portion. So you have plenty of time. Oh!" she exclaimed, pointing to the paper again. "There's one thing missing on that. I'll update it, then give you the new one. The guys have this big—huge—event planned, a gala of sorts, and you're one of the showcases. It's going to cause a big buzz for the girls' center. We're talking radio, television . . ."

Charly yawned loudly, stretching her arms and ignoring the mention of Mēkel. She couldn't help it. She didn't mean to cut Eden off or have her believe she wasn't listening, because she was. It was just that the medication was kicking her butt and her brain was hurting, and any thoughts or discussion about Mēkel would make bad worse. "Sorry. I don't mean to be rude. Can we go over it later? I have an epic headache, and I didn't sleep off the meds."

Eden smiled. "I understand. But before you crash, just give today's schedule a once-over so you can get a head start on the lineup, and mentally prep for the guys' mission to make something good out of something bad." She reached over, pointing to the paper. "See, Grime to Shine. Get it?"

Charly glanced at the paper, then nodded. She already knew why she was there, and she would do all she could to help them with their center so she didn't see a need to talk about it. Not now, anyway. Not when she felt like she did. "Got it," she said. "Got it. On it. And will fix it, as soon as I get up."

"Good, glad to hear it," Eden said, settling back in her seat. "Last thing: Do you want to stop and pick up something on the way? It's obvious you're going to need medicine that won't make you sleepy, but we've got that part covered. And the network sent over a list of your likes and needs, but you know, just in case they forgot to forward us everything that you'd want, we're not that far away from a store. I can run in and buy whatever while you nap."

Charly looked down at the paper again as if her answer was written on it. The words began to blur, and she didn't see the need to fake the funk like she was reading it. She handed the paper back to Eden, then shook her head in the negative at Eden's question. "Thanks, but I'm good. If I need something, it won't be until later. Please just wake me when we get there." She closed her eyes, settling in for the short ride.

Eden's hand was tapping her shoulder before she knew it. "Charly. Charly." Her words were soft to Charly's ears. "Charly!" she said loudly, her tone rising and filled with what sounded like panic.

Charly's eyes shot open. "Yes? What is it, Eden? You're scaring me."

A loud banging on the car made Charly jump and hit her head on the roof. They'd just crashed, she was sure.

The driver had driven too fast and had probably wrapped the SUV around something while she slept. Now the top of her head hurt. "Ouch!" she said, then looked around, seeing that they were parked. Her eyes moved to the leather seat beneath her. She'd jumped so fast and high, her purse had toppled over and its contents spilled all over. She groaned. The knocking on the car echoed through the space again, this time coming in a hip-hop beat like someone was getting ready to freestyle.

Eden shook her head, then mouthed, *Sorry.* She shrugged. "Sudden change of plans, it seems," was all she said before Lex's face was pressed against the window.

Charly's heart stopped for a split second. Not only had she not had time to rest, she hadn't had time to freshen up, and one of the finest guys she'd ever laid her eyes on was watching her. "Tell him something to make him go away, Eden. If only for a second," she urged, scrambling to find her compact. Her mouth felt dry and yucky, and her face was still coated in the dampness that had always covered her when she'd flown. She didn't know if it was because of the air pressure that killed the circulation or her always feeling closed in, but whatever it was, it needed to be washed off. *Immediately,* she thought, locating the compact.

"One second, Lex," Eden said, through the window she'd lowered a bit more than an inch.

Charly opened the compact, looked at her reflection, and groaned. Her mascara had run, and her eyes resembled a panda's. "Great," she muttered. Here she was, meeting a boxer, and she looked like she'd been beat up by one. "I look like I have two black eyes," she was saying when Lex opened the door, bent down and stuck his head inside the car.

"Charly St. James," he began, then blinked slowly and deliberately, giving her a short glance at his golden-colored eyes. He stopped. "What happened to your face?" He looked at Eden, then toward the driver, then back to Eden again. "Did someone jump on her, E? I knew I should've picked her up myself." His tone held anger. He backed out of the car, stood up, turned in a circle, then stomped his foot. He muttered curses under his breath, and Charly saw why he'd been touted as a bad boy. "That's why you never hire your people to do something for you."

"I did my job," Eden protested, then turned to Charly. "We're like family," she explained.

"Yo. Yo. Yo," Whip, the driver, said, turning around and lowering the window. "My job is to drive, and if anything happened to her it was *before* we saw her." He put up his hands in surrender. "And not because we got in an accident. I don't crash anymore."

Lex squatted next to the open car door again, then stuck one long and muscular arm inside, moving his open palm toward Charly. "Come on, Charly. Let's get you iced up." He looked at Eden. "Y'all know I can't fight in the street anymore, not since they registered my hands as weapons." He looked toward the front of the SUV. "One swing and I go to jail and no more professional boxing for me, according to the boxing commission." He turned his attention back to Eden. "But I'll tell you what, E," he said. "Whoever blacked her eyes . . . I'm going to give them more than a hit, I'm going to knock them out," he spat.

Charly almost laughed at his saying blacked instead of blackened, but his being convinced she had been beat up stopped her. *Great! Now I know I really look like I've been in a fight,* whirled through her mind, followed by what Eden had said about being like family to Lex. That could prove to be a good thing or just the opposite.

4

Charly was grumpy, and her irritation grew by the second. Stride after stride, one of her sneaker-clad feet connected to her butt, and she wasn't too thrilled about what she felt like she was being forced to do. She hadn't even made it past the guest cottage's foyer, and Lex was urging her to hurry, despite her telling him about her allergies. He insisted her seasonal issues couldn't happen in Las Vegas because there was more sand than greenery. Making things worse, though she'd sworn she hadn't been in a fight, he was still adamant that she had been, swearing that nothing slowed down adrenaline pumping through your veins more than a long, fast, and hard run.

Her eyes hadn't been blackened by a fist, but by cheap mascara she'd purchased at the last minute that, obviously, wasn't waterproof. The rings around her eyes were proof that the drugstore makeup couldn't survive con-

tinuous yawns that had made her eyes water. Not only
hadn't Lex believed her, he hadn't felt sorry for her
either, that was for sure. He'd been set on her joining
him for a workout, which, she'd discovered when she entered the guest cottage, he'd had planned all along. Either
he or his people had draped what someone considered
exercise clothes over a bench in the foyer, and she'd
changed into them in a hallway bathroom. She hadn't
even seen her sleeping quarters, never mind gotten to
take a powernap.

Now she was positioned behind Lex on a hill that
stretched higher than her eyes could see. There seemed to
be no end in sight, and she wondered if he'd flown her
out to kill her from overexertion. She was a reality television star, but not one who was on a weight-loss show, so
she didn't see the need to work out like he did.

"C'mon, Charly baby," Lex urged, running in front of
her. His calf muscles tightened with each stride, and she
wished he'd unroll his sweat pants to cover his legs. It
was just too hard to concentrate on the earth beneath her
with his chiseled cuts snatching her attention. "You don't
have a physique like that for nothing, Charly baby.
Everything about you just looks like you work out." He
continued to jog uphill, pulling a huge truck tire, which
was attached to his waist by a thick chain encircling it.

Charly just shook her head. She'd had no idea that
boxers ran so much, and his having what looked like a
huge dog chain wrapped around his waist only made her
appreciate his athleticism more. She didn't know how he
did it, but he was doing it with such ease she could tell it
was something he often did. "I . . . do . . . work . . . out,"

she sputtered, out of breath, then stopped and bent over. She couldn't keep up any longer, and wasn't embarrassed about it. She put her hands on her knees, then dropped them on the ground. She pressed her palms against the sandy dirt on either side of her feet, stretching her body and catching her wind. She was in a full bend with the top of her head on her shoes.

"Ahh. A yogi?" Lex said, looking down at her and jogging in place.

She hadn't even heard him turn around and make his way to her, but there he was, looking upside down because her head was. "Not a full-fledged one, but I partake here and there. I was introduced to it a couple of seasons ago, and now I can't help it," she admitted, closing her eyes. His feet in constant motion caused the dirt to stir, and it was swirling toward her eyes.

He stopped running in place. "Sorry for kicking dirt in your face. Constant motion is a habit. When you run, you run. There's no time to stand still—inside or outside of the ring. So what kind of yoga do you do? Power? Hot? Hatha?" he asked, switching the topic off of himself and back to Charly.

Charly unfolded her body, then stretched her arms behind her head, smiling. Someone in Lex's position—world-renowned public persona—would usually be so full of ego that they only wanted to talk about themselves. *Humble and cute*, she thought, her grin widening. Even though he was off by a mark, his being versed in yoga also impressed her, especially because of his reported bad-boy-from-the-hood reputation, which was hard for her to see. He didn't seem like a bad anything.

She brought her hands together above her head, then folded again. "Familiar with yoga, I see," she said.

Lex followed suit, bending over, the long chain still secured around his waist. Surprisingly, even with a tire attached to him, he could touch his head to his knees. "I'm a real athlete. I'm familiar with all kinds of cross training, especially sports that help me relax and stretch out my muscles. I can't afford to get a cramp in the ring."

Charly nodded. He had a point. "I do Ashtanga. But I think they're all considered Hatha. At least the ones you mentioned, but I could be wrong, so don't take it as gospel," she said, her eyes on her ankles. She exhaled loudly, then stood.

Mimicking her again, Lex laughed. He rubbed the side of his face, then bit his bottom lip. "I guess your Darth Vader breathing should've given you away."

She joined him in laughter, now more impressed than before. He had to have been in an Ashtanga class or known someone who practiced it, because that's exactly what she'd thought they all sounded like too when she first heard the Ashtanga yogis.

"Good one, and so true. Unfortunately, I can't give full credit to Ashtanga breathing. Today, I have to blame my stuffy nose—that's the reason I sound so loud. Allergies. So how many more blocks do we have to run before we call it a wrap?" She reached her arms above her head, put her palms together, and stood tall, making sure to keep her shoulders relaxed.

"Sun Salute asanas," Lex stated, naming the yoga postures. Then he switched gears again. "Don't tell anyone I know all of this yoga stuff. They may think I'm soft." He winked. "You mean how many more miles do we have to run?" he asked, then motioned his hand toward their surroundings. The rugged path was just that, and it was bordered by desert and occasional greenery. "No blocks here, Charly baby. In my old spot on the other side of the city, I ran on some back roads, but here, it's just me and these hills. That's what I love about this new place—no interruptions and complete privacy. It's no finding this camp if you don't know where you're going. We're kinda off the radar." He looked appreciative. "But I do hit the streets when I'm back on the Eastside of L.A., though. I grew up around there, in South Central. My pops doesn't believe in giving up the hood, he says it keeps us grounded and tough. Oh, and you don't have allergies. You have a cold."

"I have allergies, not a cold. How could you know that?" Charly began moving in place. She'd warmed her muscles with the Sun Salute, but now she needed to get her adrenaline pumping again so she could push through to the end of her and Lex's run.

"I bet you you do have a cold, and I'll also up the bet. I bet you dinner that I can cure it. You in?" Lex said.

Charly smiled. "Okay. Whatever. Now back to what I was saying before you became a doctor. You should try it sometime—running on the street here. It's cleaner," she said, then took off at a slow pace, as fast as her burning thighs would allow.

A loud, shrill sound cut through the air, stopping her in her tracks. Charly turned, then shook her head. Lex stood feet behind her with interest dancing in his eyes and his index and pinky fingers stuck in the corners of his mouth. He was whistling louder than she'd ever heard anyone whistle. "Not up, but this way, Charly. We're going back down the hill."

"Really?" she asked, ready to take it all the way to the top. Yes, she was tired and sore and ready to quit, but she couldn't. Despite her allergies—and it was allergies, despite Lex believing otherwise—kicking her butt, she was never one to give in. She didn't plan on stopping now. "But I thought we were just getting started," she said, teasing and flirting.

Lex just laughed, adjusting the chain around his waist. "I completed my morning workout at five a.m. I was just doing this to see how committed you are," he admitted, confirming what her gut had told her when she'd first laid eyes on the exercise clothes. She threw him a dirty look; then he stilled himself, positioning his body like he was waiting to take a hit. Charly obliged him, quickly bounding toward him and punching him in an arm that felt like steel.

"Oww." He feigned hurt, then rubbed his solid bicep where she'd connected her dainty fist. "I guess I better be careful. I saw the video of you beating up Mēkel online, so I know you're not to be played with. Why you have to be so hard on my boy? You know he's a pretty boy. He's the lover, I'm the fighter," he teased.

Charly rolled her eyes, dismissing the video. "So you had me run because you just wanted to see me sweat, and admire me in these . . . these clothes, if you can even call them that?" she asked, deadpan. The T-shirt and shorts she wore were purposely faded and looked toddler sized. She pulled on the bottoms, making them snap back against her skin, then adjusted the shirt that read TEAM "GOLDEN BOY" LEX across her chest in stylish, funky blue letters. Her eyes moved down to her feet. "I see someone likes to see his name in print. But I gotta admit I like the sneakers. I'll definitely rock these again. Can't say the same for these baby clothes though." She shook her head. "You should stick to boxing; fashion is not your forte."

Lex painted his face with hurt. He held his hand over his heart, dropped his head, then gazed up at her with golden eyes—the same liquid golds that had earned him his nickname. "Whaddya mean? You don't want to be on my team, Charly?" His question was laced with flirtation, but the real interest behind his words was obvious.

Charly sauntered past him, allowing the slope of the hill to move her faster. "I don't do teams, Lex. I'm a one-woman show. I thought you knew," she spat sassily, meaning every word.

"Oh, I know. That's why I said it and made the bet," he mumbled under his breath, apparently thinking Charly hadn't heard him. "A one-woman show? Is that right?" he asked in a louder tone, catching up.

"No, Lex. Not just right, one-hundred," she said, making it clear that she was one-hundred percent on the up-and-up with him. She tried to keep her hips from swaying so hard, but the steep hill was making it difficult not to do so. She stopped, then turned. "Let's get something clear, Golden Boy. I may be in the company of one of the greatest fighters of all time, but you, you're finally in the company of equality. I'm afraid we weren't properly introduced," she said, extending her hand. "Let's start over."

Lex's golden eyes danced and he nodded. He took her proffered hand, dwarfing it in his huge one. "I'm Lex, better known as Golden Boy," he said with more than a little ego puffing his demeanor. "But you, pretty, pretty Charly, the one-woman show, can call me Lex." He bit his bottom lip and raked his eyes up and down her frame.

Charly stood on tiptoe to reach his chin, then pushed it up until his eyes were focused on her face instead of below her neckline. She shook his hand. "And you can call me Charly, better known as Your Match, and not your match like I'm the perfect fit for you as in mate or girlfriend or whatever. I'm your match as in your worthy opponent." She winked, nodding her head, then smiled because she'd used mate, the word Liam used to refer to friend. Here she was all the way in Las Vegas with an incredible guy like Lex, and Liam had still found a way to slip into her thoughts.

Lex bit his bottom lip again, and Charly thought she was going to pass out. She questioned how she was going to make it through the day keeping her professionalism. He was just too fine, too chiseled, too tempting. "I accept the invitation, Charly baby." He winked, almost making her melt from his flirting. "I don't care if it's on the phone, across the dinner table, working out, any way is good with me, just as long as I can call you. And you did just say I can call you, Charly." He paused, as if knowing the silence would make his statement marinate in her head. He nodded. "Remember, you invited me to. I'll see you at the bottom of the hill." He turned, then took off running with a cloud of dirty-looking smoke in his wake as he dragged the tire behind him.

Charly was about to chase or call after him, but changed her mind. She had nothing to prove; her work on the show had spoken for her. Otherwise, why would he and the other guys have requested her help on their project? With what they were worth individually, not to mention the connections that came with their star status, they could afford anyone's help with the girls' retreat. But they'd chosen her, so that confirmed her ability and credibility. "You're cute, but not that cute. Okay, maybe you are, but so am I," she said under her breath, then stopped. Another cloud of dirt floated in the air, coming her way. She covered her eyes with one hand, squinting to get a good look at the cause. "What in the . . . ?"

"Charly! Charly!" a voice was calling her, and Charly couldn't tell if it was male or female. Whatever sex it belonged to, it was loud and amplified, indicating it had to be sounding through some sort of speakers.

Charly tilted her head and focused her eyes. A steady hum of a motor met her ears, and she questioned if she was hearing things. She was up in the mountains, after all. Or what she assumed to be mountains, she told herself when she spotted a golf-cart-looking buggy climbing up her way with a tiny boy in it. She noticed he wore a set of dull grays that resembled her faded pink running gear and was in the driver's seat with a bullhorn pressed against his mouth, still calling her name. "Yes?" Charly answered.

"Charly! Charly!" the voice was still blaring.

"Hey, bruh. I'm over here!" Charly yelled back, deciding to greet whoever in a friendly manner, and "sis" had worked on her when Eden had used it. It had made her feel at ease, so she thought she'd try the family-type moniker on Mr. Bullhorn. Charly put a hand on her hip. *Clearly this dude has to be in love with his own voice*, she said to herself, a bit peeved that whoever-he-was was still calling her name after they'd locked eyes. For a second, Charly thought about asking the boy if the device was connected to his lips, then changed her mind after the dune-buggy-looking mobile came to a stop and the guy, clad in a shirt that had GOLDEN BOY TRAINER stretched across his chest, hopped out. Charly raised her arm and waved her hand in the air even though they were only feet apart. "I'm right *here*, bruh," she sang between clenched teeth.

The boy nodded, running his tiny hand over his extremely thin and curly sandy-brown hair. He walked closer to her, and she saw his smooth chocolate skin was dotted with hundreds of freckles. "I see you. I just wanted to make sure you heard me—you know, in case you had on headsets," he said. His words were dry and flat, and his unhappy tone said he was clearly lying. "I've been sent to get you so you don't get lost." He looked back at Charly. "I'm Bopsy, one of the trainers in Lex's camp," Charly thought she heard him say.

"Bopsy?" Charly questioned, following behind. She hadn't even been here a full day, and already she was bumping heads with somebody. She could already hear Liam's mouth chastising her about not liking someone and her explaining that she was not at fault, which he'd never believe. *Maybe his tone isn't as nasty as I think, and I'm just tired*, she tried to convince herself. She did have a habit of reaching a state of irritation quicker when she was sleep deprived.

"No, not *Bop*sy. I said *Bob*sy—with two b's. Bobsy because I'm nasty with my bob and weave—like in boxing. You are familiar with boxing, right?" Bobsy said haughtily, as to say, *Try me if you want.* "Hop in."

No, she couldn't blame her disdain for this Bobsy-with-two-b's dude on her lack of sleep or being overmedicated. She flat-out didn't like the boy's attitude. "Well, two-b's-Bobsy, to answer your question, I'm versed in all kinds of fighting—street and ring. In fact, I'm fluent," Charly pointed out, then got into the dune-buggy-looking vehicle. She held her head high, remembering who was who. Bobsy was a trainer, but he must've been a gopher too because he'd been sent to retrieve her. "When we stop, I'd appreciate a bottle of water," Charly said, letting Bobsy know his place.

5

They were waiting for her, Charly discovered when the off-road vehicle, as Bobsy had called it, neared the bottom of the hill. They hung a right, veering onto a blacktop path that encircled Lex's gated property, but, thankfully, wasn't close enough for the guys to see her face. She guessed there had to be at least a half block's worth of land between the front of the guest cottage and the trail. But the guys were definitely there. It wasn't the small gathering in front of the house that gave them away, nor was it the expensive car that she guessed was a Maserati from the sleek body design and butterfly doors; it was Mēkel's raspy tenor riding a funky mid-tempo track, on one of the most incredible songs Charly had ever heard. As much as she hated to admit it, his voice was beautiful, and whatever the name of the song was, it was guaranteed to make crowds wild out. This Charly was certain of, because she was already hypnotized and ready to party, and she hadn't even heard the full length yet.

"That's hot," Bobsy said, referring to the song.

Charly ignored him, more interested in the warm breeze that blew her way, carrying a funky scent. She cringed. She was hot, sticky, and sweaty. She raised her arm and took a quick whiff, then shook her head. She was also musty, and that wouldn't do. She leaned over. "Can you take me to the back door?" she asked Bobsy.

Bobsy turned and eyed Charly with a half-sneer. "Nope."

Charly reared back her head, ready to spew venom, then caught herself. She needed Bobsy now, and knew that getting nasty with Bobsy wasn't going to get her anywhere, so she opted instead for sweetness. She smiled, remembering some old adage about it being easier to catch a bee with sugar, not vinegar. *And Bobsy's definitely acting like a male bee*, Charly thought. *But not like the insect.* "C'mon, Bobsy. I'm tired and I just want to shower. Please take me to the back door," she sang.

Bobsy threw her a look, still nodding to the music that could still be heard in the distance. "I said nope because I can't. There's no back door to take you to. There's the front door, then there's the side door, but you can see it from the front. Hard to explain, but you'll see it when we get closer. Either way, there's no getting around the crew, if that's what you're trying to do."

"That's exactly what I'm trying to do. How am I supposed to make a good impression—look like I'm capable of helping with the project, looking like this? This is for the girls," she mumbled. "It's not about me. Never was. This is for girls who need help and support," she continued, talking to herself. If the girls the guys had come together to support were battling and surviving life-threatening illnesses, surely she could endure the guys seeing her sweaty and funky.

The off-road vehicle jerked to a sudden stop. "What did you just say?" Bobsy asked, pressing the brake. "You know, about the girls?"

Charly exhaled. "I wasn't talking to you, Bobsy. I was talking to myself."

Bobsy turned around in the seat and faced Charly. "I know who you were talking to. Can you repeat it? Please? You said it wasn't about you?" Bobsy asked, giving Charly the same bootleg sugarcoated tone that Charly had tried to use as bait.

"It's not. I said it never was, and I also said, this is for the girls. I'm doing this to aid girls. In short, I was reminding myself that this trip isn't about me—it's not a vacation or me having me-time or even me getting to be around the guys—I'm here to help others who are dealing with more than sweat and being uncomfortable, so it shouldn't matter that I stink or that I have to face Lex and whoever else is here to meet me when I get out of this contraption. Happy?" She sneered.

The dune buggy zipped onward without warning from Bobsy. Charly's head wobbled from the sudden movement, and she was seconds away from letting Bobsy have it. She didn't know what this dude's problem was, but knew Bobsy had better fix it before she was forced to. Bobsy turned toward the guest cottage, then threw Charly another look. "I wouldn't say I'm happy, Charly. But I'll admit when I'm not right about something."

"You mean you'll admit when you're wrong about something?"

Bobsy's head shook in the negative. "No, because I'm never wrong . . . it's just sometimes I'm not right." The vehicle zipped toward the side of the guest cottage, out of the guys' view, then wheeled across the grass and stopped. "I'll go distract everyone while you go in through the butler's pantry." Bobsy pointed toward tall plants and palm trees. "The entrance is through there, just behind the shrubs and flowers. Just push them out of your way, and you'll see it . . . and the crew won't see you. There are too many plants."

"Thanks, Bobsy," Charly said, hopping out and fixing her clingy, sweaty clothes, hoping she didn't run into the butler and wondering why she hadn't seen one when she'd first arrived. She took another whiff of her underarms, and almost knocked herself out. She was never one to sweat the way she was here in Las Vegas, and walking around smelling like vegetable soup had never been a problem for her before. She'd always smelled good. She guessed she just needed to adjust to the weather and invest in some better, perhaps clinical, deodorant.

"Oh, and Charly? One more thing," Bobsy said, turning sideways to face Charly with arms crossed over his chest.

Charly turned and locked eyes with her nemesis, though she didn't know why he had become her opponent. "Yes?"

"Just because I'm helping you out doesn't make us friends," Bobsy said without the least bit of hesitation.

Charly laughed and shook her head. She turned to face Bobsy, wearing a look of contempt and disgust. "Well, Bobsy, let's put it this way. I'm so not surprised, and so very grateful to hear you say that. I've had enough fake friends in my lifetime. I don't do wishy-washy people—especially ones who have a problem with others for no reason." Her lips turned up into a smile, which was fueled by a thought. "A bit of advice. People usually dislike people they don't know because there's something about the other person that reminds them of themselves—usually that person possesses something the person doesn't like about themselves or wishes they had. Sometimes it's as simple as achievement, a thing anyone can accomplish with focus and hard work. I don't know the whys. Jealousy, envy? Possibly. Is it sad and pitiful? Definitely. Strange thing is, I usually encounter uncalled-for nasty attitudes from girls. You're the first guy." She shrugged. "Oh, and one other thing. Don't forget my water." With that, Charly walked away. She didn't have time for any more Bobsys in her world. She had entertained enough nonsense and unnecessary dramatics, and wouldn't do it again. Besides, she told herself, this Bobsy boy had serious boxing skills, abilities that Charly knew she would have to prepare for if she were to take him on. But she could if she had to, she thought. They were close to the same size.

"I'm here to build up people, not tear 'em down," she reminded herself, making her way to the side entrance.

* * *

"There you are. The alarm said the butler's pantry door opened, but I didn't expect you. I'm glad you're here though. Time's ticking." Eden tapped her watch as soon as Charly made her way inside the door. She then dug into her pocket and retrieved an envelope and handed it to Charly. "I apologize. I was supposed to give this to you after you landed. Please don't tell Lex that I forgot. When it comes to you being here and the project they have planned for the girls, he wants everything to be perfect. I don't blame him. He should." She raised her brows. "Unfortunately, I can't always be perfect, or, unfortunately, remember the guys' requests either, for that matter."

Charly stood still for a second, welcoming the central air of the guest cottage, her body cooling in the breezy circulation. She took a look at herself clad with sweaty clothes, and hated the feeling of being coated in yucky perspiration. "Me either. I'm not always perfect either—can't you tell?" She grinned and accepted the envelope. She exhaled. Her breath came out in a long, loud whoosh. She slipped her index finger under the flap, and tore open the thick ecru paper. She pulled out a card, opened it, then tensed when she read the message.

Charly, I hope you're ready. Lives will change because of you, mama. Everything you're down for, I'm down for, and we're counting on you. Let's raise these girls up until they blow up in a good way. Let's get this thing moving. I know you won't let the girls or us down. –Faizon

Charly closed her eyes, thinking about Faizon's words. Knowing that lives could change because of her and that the guys were counting on her was heavy, and already she could feel the pressure. She didn't want to let anyone down. She exhaled again, then ran her hand over her ponytail.

"Are you all right, Charly? You seem a bit frustrated," Eden said, crossing her arms and leaning against a pillar. "You know you can talk to me about anything, and, I promise it'll never go further than us. I'm good at secrets. Very." She nodded, impressed with herself.

Charly pursed her lips together, then mimicked Eden's head nod. She was a doer, not a talker, so she'd let her actions speak for her, including finding an outlet to relieve herself of the pressure that came with her assignment. "Thanks, Eden. I appreciate it. I'm good, though. However, I'll keep in mind your great secret-keeping ability. I may need it one day." She winked. "I'm cool. I just need to shower and change, and, eventually, get some rest. Where's my room?"

"Your room?" Eden's eyebrows drew together. "Oh, that's right. You didn't see it earlier because you had to rush and change to go run." She shook her head. "You may want to get used to that. Being rushed, I mean. Lex has a way of making people move like he does. Lightning fast."

Charly nodded, making a mental note about Lex. She'd rushed and changed in the hallway bath once because of him, but she wasn't going to allow him to make it a habit. "Got it. But I'm not going to let him rush me into anything. I don't work for him; I'm here to work on something with him. That's not the same thing. So . . ." She pursed her lips, waiting for direction. "Can you please tell me where my room is? I need to hurry and unpack. Maybe take a cold shower to help me wake up. I don't want to leave anybody waiting too long, and I don't want to nod off during our meeting." She laughed a little, then stretched and yawned.

"I already unpacked and put away your things. You have some really nice purses and shoes. I hope you don't mind. Lex demanded it. You're not to really move a finger while you're here. He wants you to be able to focus on the task at hand." She pointed toward the other side of the house. "Your room is over there, just through the double doors off of the main living area. It's the second door to the right down the hall. You won't miss it," Eden said. "But before you go, follow me over here to the kitchen. I was just about to grab Lex and the others something to drink. He asked me to give you something too." She moved her index finger toward what Charly assumed was the kitchen area.

"The others?" Charly repeated, unsure of who was gathered out front. She could see a group surrounding the car, but didn't know if they were helping with the project or not.

Eden nodded. "Yes, Lex's crew. His other crew, trainers mostly, but Faizon and some of the others who are assisting with the landscaping part of the project will be here tomorrow. After that, Faizon will be in and out because he has to be on set for a movie shooting. And Mēkel . . ."

She shook her head in question and shrugged. "He's recording, and when he records, he can disappear into the studio for months, but he should surface soon. Hopefully," she said, throwing Charly a knowing look. "But all three of them are super close. They've been like brothers for years." She clapped her hands. "Now let's get you the good stuff. It's what Lex wants you to have, and I guarantee you it'll pick you up. Lex and the trainers swear by it, and even Bobsy, who hates the taste of almost everything, likes it so you know it's a winner." She walked across the marble floor, her heels clacking with each step, then pushed through a swing door.

Charly shrugged her shoulders when Eden wasn't looking. She was glad she wouldn't see Mēkel, and couldn't care less what Bobsy thought about anything. "Whatever it takes," Charly said, following her into a tastefully decorated immaculate space that served as an open kitchen and den. She leaned on the island's granite countertop, wanting to lay her head on the coolness. "Where's the butler? I didn't see him in the pantry."

Eden laughed and opened the Sub-Zero fridge. "You're really funny, Charly. I guess a butler should come with a butler pantry. I don't know why they call them that." She bent over and stuck her head inside one of the refrigerator's glass double doors. She was moving her arms around, obviously looking for something. "Aha. Here it is," she said, backing out of the icebox with a bottle in her hand. "This is the flavor that I recommend above the others. It's Lex's sports drink. It'll hit markets and vitamin stores in a couple of weeks, then will be released internationally."

She turned around and handed a nicely wrapped, black-colored bottle to Charly.

Charly ruffled her brows, looking at the bottle. She was glad Eden had taken her ignorance of a butler pantry not having a real living butler as a joke. "I don't like drinking or eating anything that I can't see, and you definitely can't see through this," she said, twisting the cap until she heard the seal break. She put it to her nose, and took a slight whiff. It smelled good. "Kind of flowery, kind of fruity."

Eden nodded. "Yes and yes. It's all-natural, of course, and it has some botanicals and fruit. However, the main ingredients are vitamins, herbs . . . plant extracts—that's why it's in a dark bottle, to keep the flavors and maintain the strength of the good stuff. There's nothing in there that isn't from the earth. But what else would you expect from a tree-hugger?" She laughed. "Lex is vegan, you know. All the way down to his boxing gloves and boxing shoes. No leather, no animal byproducts. Nothing."

Charly nodded, impressed. *A vegan bad boy.* She really dug Lex's lifestyle, but not enough to make it her own. "Does he really drink this?"

Eden nodded. "Sure. In fact, his father's family has been brewing it forever. It's Lex's special recipe, and one of the reasons he has so much energy in the ring."

The bottle rim was pressed to her lips and she was gulping the juice mixture down before she knew it. If it was natural and gave Lex energy, she knew she couldn't do anything else but benefit from it.

"Hold it. Hold it!" Eden said, grabbing Charly's hand

and pulling it away from her mouth, causing the juice to spill and dribble down Charly's chin. "It's super strong. You're not supposed to drink it all at once."

Charly wiped her chin with the back of her hand, then belched. She smiled big and wide. "Too late."

6

Her heart was racing. Speeding. Going one hundred and eighty miles per hour in a sixty-mile-per-hour zone. Charly grabbed the sides of her head, then put a hand on her chest, then took her index and middle fingers and laid them across the inside of her wrist. She had to check her pulse. "Whew. It's off the meter!" she said, then grabbed her toiletry bag and cell phone and made her way into the en suite bathroom that was situated off of the fabulous bedroom she was staying in during her visit. The suite was laid out in plush fabrics and furniture that screamed expensive, and she couldn't help but touch them. As her travels had taken her across the States, she'd bunked in some of the most luxurious hotels and grown accustomed to finer things, but she'd never before seen the richness that was throughout Lex's guest cottage. "Handmade furnishings. Has to be," she determined, speed walking across the wet-looking marble navy floor that mirrored the deep blue ceiling above, which she noticed had the zodiac painted in a perfect golden circle. She set her toiletry bag on the marble-topped sink, grabbed the thickest bath towel she'd ever touched from a bar on the wall, and carefully rested her phone on a nearby built-in teak shelf. Reaching in to turn on the spray, she stopped. There were nine huge circular disks with spray holes in them; one gigantic one on top, and four on either side. She laughed. The rain shower resembled an automatic car wash. Then something else caught her eye. There was a waterproof docking system on the wall, housed in an enclosure. Upon closer inspection, she realized it would fit her phone. She nodded her head in approval and grabbed her cell. She docked it, selected her favorite playlist, then safeguarded it behind the wrapped glass casing. "Voila!" she said, then turned the temperature dial to medium heat and opened the spigots. Jumping back to prevent herself from getting splashed by the massive spray she'd just unleashed, she accidentally dropped the bath towel. Reaching down to get it, she now saw the constellations that were above were also on the floor too. As she ran her finger over one, she discovered it was just a reflection from the ceiling. "Wow, as above, so below. Hermetic," she said, then caught herself. A design reflecting wasn't such a big deal, and she knew her over-the-top impression had probably been caused by the adrenaline rushing through her veins. Ever since Lex's athletic juice had kicked her system into fast gear, she hadn't been her normal self. Her movements were quick. Her brain was zipping from one thought to another. Every detail was magnified. "There has to be something in that juice, and it can't be natural, either. Not the way I'm zipping around and sweating," she said, disrobing and hopping into the human carwash at top speed.

Covered in bubbles, she was dancing and singing at the top of her lungs when the playlist was interrupted by a new Mēkel single. It was Liam's special ringtone, which she'd forgotten to change after her run-in with the chart-topper. "Ugh!" Charly stopped. She squinted her eyes, careful not to let the suds seep between her lashes. Reaching out her soapy fingers to pop open the enclosure so she could answer and make Mēkel's powerful voice go away, she tried to convince herself that his raspy tenor wasn't appealing, but she couldn't. Every note he hit, every word he sang, was as delicious now as it had been before he'd ticked her off. "Whatever. Oops." Moving her wet and slippery fingers too fast, she fumbled. "Slow it down," she chastised herself, then took her time, finally selecting ACCEPT.

"Hey love." Liam's voice boomed like a nuclear explosion through the bathroom's surround-sound speakers, making Charly jump from the vibrating bass.

She already had an anxious feeling throughout her body, and his blasting voice only made her jitter more. "One sec," she said, trying to turn down the volume. Her wet fingertips moved wildly until she was certain she had pressed the correct button. "You there?" she asked, closing the plastic enclosure.

Liam's laugh sounded; this time his tone and volume were more acceptable, and no longer blaring. "Yes, love. I'm here, and it seems I'm there too. Ooh la la. Seems you've really taken to the bubbles."

Charly's eyes widened in panic, and a burning sensation set in. She groaned, reaching for something to wipe the soap from her face. "Oh. God!" she screamed. If Liam knew she was covered in bubbles that could only mean one thing. "You can see me, Liam?" She dropped to her knees, embarrassed.

Liam laughed. "Yes!" he continued to giggle. "There, there, love. No need to panic. I could only see your face and neck. Promise. Where'd you go? Come back. I can't see you anymore."

Charly stayed in her crouching position. There was no way she was going to stand without being sure Liam couldn't see more than he'd admitted to. Sure, she would be able to see what he saw on the minuscule screen within the main screen, but in order to do so she'd have to risk exposing herself. That she wasn't willing to do. "Hang up, Liam!" she screamed. "Hang up! I'll call you back in two seconds."

"Aww, c'mon, love. I told you I didn't see anything." He laughed again, then conceded. "Okay. If it makes you more comfortable, have it your way. I've already learned to live with suffering, working so close with you and yet not being able to really have you," he said, then hung up.

Her panic almost prevented her from finishing her shower. Worrying that Liam had seen too much of her, she had a hard time concentrating. Her heart was still rapidly beating, her body refused to slow down, and even though she was under a spray of water, she was sweating bullets. She hopped out of the stall, zipping to and fro, from towel bar to sink to clothes. She'd lost control, and knew the juice had everything to do with it. Her fingers were moving so quickly she couldn't tell that they didn't have their own brain, and, in a way, she was thankful. If the whole getting-dressed scenario were up to her—the way it normally was—she'd have failed. Epically. Without the rush, she would've been too discombobulated to complete the everyday task on time, and she was definitely under clock pressure knowing she needed to work out the project plans with Lex, then outline ones she thought would appeal to Faizon's profession. Finally, thanks to her "mind of their own" hands, as she now referred to them, she completed her getting-fabulous-for-the-sizzling-hot-boy mission, aka being the cutest she could. Pivoting in the mirror, she raised her brows in awe. Somehow, even in a simple tank dress, she had upped her usual style, and in fewer than fifteen minutes—a world record, as far as she was concerned. She even had Liam back on the cell.

"So, you still don't believe me?" he was saying, just as she was checking her pulse again.

"Oh my gosh, Liam. I'm *so* high," Charly sung into the phone, while wiggling her nose. Her heart was racing, her eyes were wide, and, though she'd been set on much-needed rest earlier, she couldn't have gone to sleep now if someone paid her to. "I can't stop moving. Can't stop talking. I can't stop. Can't stop." She laughed, then began dancing in place. "Like the old Bad Boy song. I thought I told you that I can't stop. Thought I told you that I won't stop," she sang, changing the lyrics. "Guess it's my own song, right? You can't really change someone's lyrics and still call the song theirs," she rattled.

"What, love? Slow down. Slow down, Charly!" Liam

yelled. "What do you mean you're high? High how? Off life, I hope."

"Not high *high*, Liam," she tried to explain. "I was just so tired. The allergy medicine, the run, the lack of sleep, you name it, it wore me out, so Eden—she's my guardian who's really Lex's family, which he doesn't seem to be too happy with if you ask me, but I guess you're not asking me..." She was rattling again, this time at a thousand miles per hour.

"Stop! Stop! Charly. Take it from the top. What about this Eden character?" Concern filled Liam's voice.

"Eden. Fabulous Eden. You'll really like her. Anyway, I was so tired, and she gave me something to help me wake up because we have a lot of work to do today, and because Lex told her to." She stopped, then gasped for breath. "Oh god. I have a full schedule, and here I am talking to you. I really gotta go, Liam," she was saying as she reached to end the call.

"Charly! Wait... before you hang up," Liam said, out of breath. "What did this Eden character give you?"

Charly laughed. "Just some juice. And it must've been laced with something," she began jokingly, then reared back her head when she realized she couldn't finish her statement. Liam had hung up in her face.

A knock on the door told her it was time to get back to work.

"Yes, come in," Charly called out, slipping her feet into a funky pair of flat sandals, deciding to forego her usual boots or heels. It wouldn't be a good idea to house her feet in shin-height leather in such hot weather, or be so high up in the air moving at the pace she was—plus her soles weren't too comfy after running. Besides, she told herself, they were meeting to discuss the project, not hang out, so she didn't need to be dressed to the hilt. "This will do," she whispered to herself, giving herself the once-over as the door opened.

"Oh, what you're wearing isn't going to work, Charly. Not if you're working today. That might not be good for the promotional event either, but you'll have to check with Eden on that," a voice said nicely.

Charly looked up, her eyes wide with shock, which she would've blamed on the juice, but couldn't. She'd stretched her eyes because the nice voice belonged to Bobsy. "What's the plan for today? And when's the promotional event?" She questioned the supposed event, the sincerity of the messenger, and her now-foggy memory. She was put off by Bobsy's niceness. The dude had a straight attitude earlier, so she doubted the sudden shift in his demeanor.

Bobsy stuck a hand though the door. "Here, I think people call this a peace offering, right?" he said, holding a bottle of water. "Sorry about earlier. I woke up with a terrible headache, and it's normally not my job to do anything besides helping with training or other things related to the camp—not the guests, so Lex having me chasing after you . . . well, it didn't sit too well with me. I'm not a flunky. You get it, right?" He was smiling and shrugging, and he looked apologetic.

Charly blinked twice, hesitating before she took the water. She only took a couple of seconds to consider if she would believe Bobsy or not before deciding that Bobsy's sincerity really didn't matter that much to her.

She wasn't here for Bobsy; she was here on business. "Thanks," she said, accepting the water. "Now what were you saying about today?"

"You mind?" Bobsy asked, gesturing toward the room.

"It's cool," Charly said, curious.

Bobsy walked in, but still kept some distance between them, standing just inside the doorway. "It's just land-scaping today, but that won't start for a couple of hours. I guess the bulldozers have to finish leveling the land. Nothing you're required to do. The promotional event for girls is first thing in the morning. You're going to have to get down to the nitty-gritty, as Lex's pops would put it. You know, grime to shine? And knowing the guys' publicists, I'm sure it'll be televised. So you might want to rethink the sandals." He shrugged. "Just a heads-up."

Charly nodded, remembering Eden mentioning some-thing about a gala for girls, and knew Bobsy had a point. She couldn't show up to that event dressed down, espe-cially since it was promoting the guys' project of aiding girls who were fighting for their lives—a major mission that required Charly's beauty and design skills to make them look as good on the outside as they wanted to feel on the inside. "Yes, proper dress is key," she said, more to herself than Bobsy. Then she grabbed her cell, opened her calendar, and entered the gala event into the next morning's schedule. She put it down, slipping out of her sandals and thinking of what she could wear to do yard work today and what she could rock tomorrow for the event. She exhaled, suddenly feeling her energy drain and a hint of a headache brewing. "I know I keep saying this, but I can't help sell an idea if I don't look like the idea." She yawned, then grabbed her temples, which started throbbing when she stretched her mouth. "Right?"

Bobsy nodded in agreement. "Eden has to roll with the guys to set up. She'll be working on some things for the event in the morning, while some of the landscapers work on yard and the masons finish the new fence, so she sends her apologies. She'll meet you there, and Lex's dad will take you. An even bigger heads-up: be ready and on time. Lex's dad waits for no one, and I have some trainer stuff to take care of, so I can't go," Bobsy added.

" 'K." Charly pivoted and put her index finger to her lips. She cringed, holding the sides of her head. The room started moving. Closing her lids for a second, she tried to still it. Her sudden dizziness combined with extreme exhaustion told her Lex's magic juice had worn off and she was crashing from her herbal high. "Not now," she chastised herself. "I can't be tired now!"

She diverted her attention to the task at hand. "What to wear? What to wear? What to wear?" She paused, flashes of the clothes she'd brought with her moving through her mind, but she couldn't mentally put an outfit together, not with the room spinning, her brain banging, and her feeling as though someone had sucked the life out of her. Droplets of sweat cascaded down her forehead, and she suddenly felt an internal chill.

"Bobsy, you did say two hours, right? Do you think you can wake me in an hour? I have to lie down, and I'm too tired to trust hearing my phone's alarm."

Bobsy's head shook. "I'm not sure if I'll be finished

with my treatment in time, so I can't promise, but I'll try. I can ask Whip though. He shouldn't be busy."

"Treatment?" Charly asked, her brows crinkled together and her knees almost buckling from sudden weakness.

Bobsy's head reared back in surprise; then he stretched out his arm. "Yes, therapy. Physical. I can't help train if I'm not in tip-top training condition. It's mandatory."

Charly nodded. It made sense. "Okay, I'll just rest for a second," she told herself, looking at the clock. She stretched across the mattress.

7

Charly opened her lids and looked at the clock on the nightstand. Her lips stretched into a faint smile. She'd awoken early and on her own. She'd only closed her eyes for a couple of minutes, and already her headache was gone and the room had stopped spinning.

"Yes," she said, rolling off the bed, feeling exhilarated. Not only was she feeling better, she had an idea of what she should wear. Humming her way to the closet, she selected and slipped into a pair of jeans, a T-shirt, and the running sneakers she'd gotten from Lex. "Now, just a little bit of music," she said, grabbing her cell to play her playlist. "Oh no!" she panicked, seeing the time on the phone. 9:13 AM. Her eyes ping-ponged back and forth between her cell and the clock, then she winced when she realized the digits on the nightstand hadn't changed since she'd last looked. "It's tomorrow? Morning? Can't be!"

Her calendar alarm popped up with a reminder: *GIRLS' EVENT. DRESS TO IMPRESS!!!!!!*

With the speed of a sprinter, Charly disrobed, ran and showered, put on her makeup, combed her hair, and was back at the closet. She grabbed a yellow backless halter sundress, and a snazzy pair of five-inch heels. Within seconds, she was in the outfit and shoes, had tossed her cell into her purse and was out the door. She ran into the living area, making her way to the front door. She grabbed the knob, twisted it, then opened it with all her might, moving at top speed. "I'm dressed and ready to go," she began, then trailed off. A car could be seen driving away in the distance, and it was much too far away for her to stop it. Charly gulped. Bobsy had told her that the event was first thing this morning, but there was no way they would've left without her, she thought. She looked around, and there was no one in sight. "Oh no," she said, then dug her cell phone out of her bag. She didn't know whom she was going to call, but there had to be someone. But where would she tell them to take her? She had no idea where the event was. She snapped her fingers. Mr. Day had given her her itinerary, and it had Eden's information on it. "Yes," she said, turning around to go back into the house, but the door was locked. Charly grabbed her head in frustration, then remembered the other entrance. She exhaled, praying she could get in, then moved quickly toward the side door. Before she made it, she heard a vehicle zooming nearby with a 2 Chainz song blasting.

"Whip!" Charly said, feeling her anxiousness melt. She

turned in the direction of the music, and walked as quickly as she could, yelling Whip's name at the top of her lungs, hoping he would be able to hear her.

She'd crossed the yard to the side of the guest cottage that she hadn't gone to before, and skirted a fleet of cars parked in front of a seven-car garage. She saw Whip polishing the SUV.

Whip looked up. "What's up, Charly?" he asked, bobbing his head to the track.

Charly was out of breath. "I need you. Bobsy was supposed to ask you to wake me, and I overslept . . . yesterday," she said, feeling stupid. "Anyway, I have to get to the event this morning. I can't miss that too. Can you take me? Do you know where it is?" she asked, half-scared for her life. The last time she had been in the car with Whip, he hadn't been the safest driver.

Whip shook his head in the negative. "Bobsy couldn't have asked me anything. Not this morning. I was dropping off Lex and the crew, and Lex told everybody to let you sleep so you could get over your cold. He's big on health. Anyway, it doesn't matter. I can't take you. I gotta take care of the ride. That's what Lex told me."

Charly exhaled. "Please, Whip. I think the event is more important to Lex than how much his ride gleams."

Whip wouldn't budge. "Nah . . . plus, I don't feel like anyone telling me how to drive." He rubbed the side of his face, then went back to wiping down the SUV.

"Look, Whip, I don't care how you drive. Just get me there. Quickly."

*   *   *

Charly gripped the overhead handle next to her seat, holding on for her life. The black SUV flew down the street, bouncing up and down as they encountered pothole after pothole. Looking out her window, she watched for another street sign. Already, she'd memorized three of them. She hoped that she wouldn't need to backtrack on foot to Lex's guest cottage, but she couldn't be sure, so she'd opted for the safety of knowing where she was. Whip, who'd admitted to being another one of Lex's family members, drove at top speed, taking corners, running red lights, and skidding to incomplete stops. Reckless couldn't begin to define his behind-the-wheel skills, and on more than one occasion, Charly was sure they were going to crash.

"Whew!" Whip exclaimed, pressing the brakes a little. "And another dodgeball point for us," he said, after slowing just in time to avoid the attention of a cop who, just like the other three police cars before, didn't catch him speeding. "Yes!" he exclaimed, then punched the accelerator until the wind whistled through the open windows.

"Slow down!" Charly demanded for the umpteenth time, tightening the grip on the handle to steady herself.

Whip glared at her in the rearview mirror and rolled his eyes. "Didn't I tell you I got this? You were the one running late, and I need to get you there ASAP. It's high traffic time, and this is the only way to avoid it. I need my ends, Charly, so I gotta get back and finish cleaning the rides. Lex doesn't pay for lateness. Period. Point. Blank," he said. " 'Sides, these are my streets. I know the roads and the off roads. And better than five-oh, as you can tell. So you're safe with me."

Charly's eyes widened before she could respond. Through the front window, she could see the road getting ready to end, and Whip wasn't slowing down. "There's dirt up there!" she yelled.

"Yepper. Off roads, I just told you." Whip laughed, pushing forward. "I told you I got this. But hold on. It's going to get bumpy. Shortcut!" he yelled back, still accelerating.

Charly held her breath, watching him whip the SUV as if they were on smooth highway while cranking up the music. Mēkel's voice filled the air again, and she shook her head. The sports utility vehicle bounced as they moved off the paved street and onto the rough terrain. She looked around, certain there were no streets signs in the middle of the desert. Still, though, in case she had to walk, she wanted to know how to get back. That was, if she survived the accident she was sure was about to happen. *Two trees to the far right will be on the left if I am going the other way. Water tower way up ahead. Skyscraper.* She took a mental note of the landmarks. "Whip!" she yelled when she felt the vehicle lift from the ground.

"Whew-hoo. Yayer. Didn't I tell you I am that fiyah?" he said, whipping the SUV left, and moving off the dirt and back onto a real street. "The trick is not to stop. If you stop in the desert, you may stay in the desert. Get me. That's why they call me Whip, cause I know the tricks on how to whip the whips!"

Charly exhaled and closed her eyes. She was scared

stiff, but had survived the worst, so she couldn't complain. The SUV finally moved forward at a legal pace, then turned the corner. "I see."

"Dang!" Whip yelled, banging on the steering wheel.

Sirens sounded and colorful lights flashed. Police cars zoomed in from all directions, surrounding them. "Whip, park the truck, throw the keys out the window, and get out with your hands up," a voice said over a police cruiser intercom.

Charly's brows rose as she tilted her head. "Whip, did they just say your name? Please tell me that the police don't know you by name," she said, pulling out her cell phone. With three touches of the screen, she had Liam on the line.

"Liam. Are you in or near the studio? No? Man!" She stomped her foot. She'd wanted Liam to contact the Las Vegas authorities from a studio phone and tell them who she was and why she was there, in the hopes that it would validate her story. "Don't panic, but I've been stopped by the cops again, and whatever you do, please keep this from Mr. Day," she pleaded, then listened intently as Liam instructed her to pull up the NEW YORK INDUSTRY BAD BOYS UNITE TO HELP GIRLS AT RISK article Lola had shown her, on a major newspaper's website. It had been corrected to read THE 3 HOTTEST BAD BOYS OF BOXING, R & B, AND HOLLYWOOD UNITE TO HELP TEEN GIRLS IN LAS VEGAS and now included her name. "Thanks Liam. Let's hope it works!" She ended the call.

Whip exhaled, and parked the SUV. He took the key out of the ignition, rolled down the driver's-side window, then tossed the key ring across the street. "Dang!" he said again, slowly opening the door. "Yes, they know me by name. I got my nickname because I used to be a teenage getaway driver—but that was a long time ago, Charly."

"All occupants exit the vehicle," the police said over the intercom. "Now!"

Charly froze, looking at Whip for direction. "Well?"

"Do what they say or we're both going to jail," Whip said, then hopped out of the SUV, and walked to the middle of the street with his hands raised.

Charly sat on the curb with her ankles crossed. Her elbow was resting on her knee and her chin was in her palm. She looked out into the distance, irritated and guilty. She was peeved because the cop standing over her was clearly short on brain cells, and had been asking her the same questions over and over for what seemed like an hour or more. She was filled with guilt because she'd just about twisted Whip's arm to take her to the event, and kept pushing until he'd given in. Now he was in trouble because she had been running late.

"So you're trying to tell me that you didn't know Whip is a convicted getaway driver?" the female officer, who looked like a box wearing a uniform, asked again. "He has a conditional license. He can only drive when he's working."

Charly looked up at her, and batted her eyes slowly. "I told you, he was working. He was taking me to work."

The policewoman shook her head. "Who was working? You or him? First you said he was working, then you said you were working. And the only people he's allowed to drive for are the people he works for—that's the only vehicle he's allowed to drive under court order." The woman looked her up and down. "And you're too puny to be a boxer or a trainer. What are you, fifteen?"

Charly shook her head. They kept going over the same thing, and again and again the woman couldn't put two forms of work together. "Miss, like I told you a thousand times, if you'd go look at my phone, which I gave to the other officer before you got here, it'll prove who I am. And my identification is in my purse in the truck. I already told him, and he had no problem with my statement. Why do you?"

The officer crossed her arms. "Well, that's him, and this is me." She pointed to her chest. "And now that I'm here, you're under my authority. A male cop should always call a female cop to the scene if there's a female minor involved. He can't frisk you the way I can."

Charly jumped up from the curb. "Who are you going to frisk? You can't frisk me. I'm a minor, and I'm not under arrest. What law did I break? Riding in a car that the court has given him permission to drive?" Charly turned and surveyed the small crowd that had begun to gather. "Help!" she screamed at the top of her lungs. "Help! I'm being threatened by this cop. Call the news. I'm Charly from *The Extreme Dream Team*. Somebody help and make sure you tape this! I'll give a reward. Please!" she screamed as if she were in pain.

The officer reared back her head, flaring her nostrils. Then looked around. Paranoia was all over her face, and she threw up her hands in the air as if she were surrendering. "I didn't touch her!" she yelled to a male officer headed their way. From his badge and other decorations, he looked like he was her superior.

"Betty! What are you doing?" he spat.

Charly had hit a nerve. "Officer, please help me!" Charly pushed. "All we were doing is trying to get to this event for girls. An event I was hired to help with. I gave my phone to the other cop, showed him the news article—the officer who's over there with Whip. Please read it and please keep this lady away from me and my driver. She said she was going to lock us both up!" Charly looked at Betty. "And for what? Helping little girls?" She shook her head. "Bad press. Really bad press. I'm sure the news stations out here would love to get this story."

"Let her go, Betty. She's telling the truth. I read it for myself, and they both checked out. Whip was just doing his job. This time."

8

The ride to the event was quiet, and Whip drove slowly. He turned the corner, and barely drove a mile before they finally stopped. With shaking hands, Charly opened her door and breathed deeply. She had to gather herself before she threw herself into what was the rest of her day.

"Over there," Whip said, pointing. He clearly had no intention of getting out and helping her. "And thanks . . . you know, for back there. If you hadn't've pushed, I'd be in jail this time, not juvie."

"No, if I hadn't pushed you to drive me . . ." Charly nodded, then looked in the direction of the event. "So, that's it?" she asked. How was she supposed to know where "over there" was. He'd pointed and retracted his hand so quickly, she didn't see.

"Gotcha." He hopped out of the SUV, then quickly made his way to her door, opening it. "You did get me off by calling me your driver. Maybe, after Lex cools off about this, he'll tip me. He should just because I got you here in record time. It's over a thirty-minute ride. I gotcha here in under fifteen—if you subtract the one-on-one time with the cops." Whip laughed, back to his normal self.

Charly just shook her head, looking at him and smiling. She'd wondered how someone as professional as Lex had people like Whip and Bobsy in his camp. Now she knew why Whip was there; Lex was looking out for his family and keeping Whip out of trouble. Bobsy, though, was still in question. "Thanks, Whip. It was an experience," she complimented him facetiously, and slid out of the SUV, landing softly on the sidewalk. She headed in the way he'd pointed.

"Cool," Whip said from behind. "And in case you need me, you know I'll be right here. If the cops catch me driving home without one of you guys in the car, my freedom is a wrap! And when Lex finds out, I'm a wrap too! So I'm just gonna chill and deal with him when this thing is over." He laughed.

Charly stopped and looked down at her shoes, feeling them for the first time. *Stilts.* That's what it felt like she was walking on. She hadn't noticed what they'd felt like before because she'd been in a panic from running late, then dealing with the cops. Now she was aware of them. As soon as her feet connected with the ground, she'd instantly grown five inches, thanks to the high heels pushing her to model-tall height. She was that physically elevated, and emotionally too, she noted, due to making it to the event and the eagerness rushing through her. In seconds, she'd be in the company of television cameras and girls, and Faizon and Lex, whom she was most excited about.

"Hmm," she moaned, looking around and wincing at the noise of traffic and songs that filled the air. Music genres clashed, growing louder as vehicles neared her, then the volumes lowered as they made their way down the street. It was a cyclical process of R & B tunes merging with hip-hop, hip-hop fighting with hardcore rap, and dashes of old-school tracks blending into a hodgepodge of melodies that weren't too melodic. Charly shook her head as cars whizzed by. Each seemed to have a different flavor of music blaring through its speakers, and all contained passengers that she wouldn't trust. They looked like dealers, addicts, or thieves. No, she couldn't be in the right place, that's what her gut told her. Not for a celebrity event. Something was off. She turned toward Whip, who was still waiting by the SUV, and threw him a quizzical look. She was standing in front of what appeared to be a construction site, on a not-so-appealing side of town or street, which was littered and run-down, lined with buildings that had seen better days. Better structures were on the other side, so she was sure her destination had to be over there or around the corner or anywhere else, but certainly not close to where she stood. There was no way the guys were hosting anything in such an unsafe place. Not with their level of celebrity.

Whip nodded his head, then tipped his baseball hat toward the fence. "Yeah, that's the way, Charly. Right through there. I'd come help you, but you know I can't," he yelled, indicating that her destination was through an opening in a chain link fence that she guessed was over ten-feet tall. It had bright orange strips woven through the diamond shaped openings and caution signs posted on it that prevented her view of what was behind it.

"Really?" she questioned loudly, hoping to be heard over a hip-hop track, and made her way toward two metal posts that were haphazardly situated as an opening that looked anything but safe. Walking carefully, she begged her legs not to wobble when she stepped off the smooth concrete sidewalk and through the fence opening, which she thought led to the event, but it didn't. About ten feet ahead, a tall wrought-iron gate with brick columns and bushes and flowers planted in front of it, met her eyes. The beauty of it said it was new, and she exhaled, feeling better about what she was walking into, though she was still too far away to see the happenings behind the gate. The sun shone brightly, and laughter of children tickled her ears. Things suddenly didn't seem so gloomy.

Still, the dirty rocky path challenged her steadiness as she moved forward, bopping her head as the song's volume increased with each step. The cracked cement and rocks crackled and popped under her feet, making her gain more appreciation for good-quality shoes. Though she was elevated to the height of a giant in them and the rubble moved under her steps, her soles felt as if they were resting on clouds.

"What in the . . . ?" Her eyes widened. Her jaw dropped. Her knees locked, preventing her from progressing. The wind caught in her throat. The massive stretch of land that she'd finally set her vision on made her feet hurt because she knew her heels were going to stick in the grass. Already, she could feel the pain and swelling they were certain to endure, and she hadn't even crossed the event threshold.

Eden appeared between the two brick pillars, walking through the wrought-iron fence. She looked up and stopped. She smiled, putting one hand to her chest, surprised. "Wow, I was just stepping away to call you. There's too much noise back there for me to hear." She pointed behind her. "And I needed to check on you and see how you were making out. I guess Lex's formula worked. I'm glad you made it. I was starting to worry. How'd you get here?" She made her way closer to Charly.

Charly nodded, then shook her head. She looked down at the shoes she had been sure weren't going to cause her a problem, and already knew she'd predicted wrong. Sneakers would've been wiser. Her shin-high leather boots would've been more ideal. The open makeshift field was lined with animal pens, inflatable bouncing houses, and what appeared to be building construction going on behind a barricade way in the back—all on the dirty, grassless, ground with puddles of sandy mud. "Whip brought me. I was okay, but now I don't think so," she was saying as Eden neared.

"I had a feeling you'd show so I've been keeping this with me ever since I got here because you're going to need it, and, somehow, they keep disappearing. I guess people think the pink's fashionable. Here you go . . . ?" Eden said, cutting her sentence short and handing Charly a construction hat that matched the one she wore, and a matching T-shirt. "Oh." She scanned her eyes over Charly's wardrobe, then looked at her own. She was dressed in holey jeans, Timberland boots, and a pink T-shirt that read EMPOWER YOUTH: THE GRIME TO SHINE project. "I . . . I . . ." Eden stopped, clearly at a loss for words.

Charly looked down at the long, flowing halter dress she wore, then surveyed her surroundings once more before locking eyes with Eden. "What's going on, Eden? I thought this was supposed to be some sort of publicity event or something. You did say a gala." She hiked her purse on her shoulder. "And is there a place I can put this? Do we have any lockers or anything for our valuables?"

Eden nodded, then shook her head no. "You're definitely going to want to lock up that bag. It's very expensive, and I can show you where you can put it away. And yes, yesterday I did mention a gala event, but I said later, later meaning later during your visit. Not today. And this is an event for the girls. It's the guys' Youth Empowering Youth event, where the less fortunate teens, help the even less fortunate children." She turned, moving her hand through the air. "Back through there—you might be able to see if you tiptoe—the crew and some of our girls, the ones who've battled and won. Everyone has on pink, and the assistants have on red shirts. The girls are here helping; they're giving back by working on the Grime to Shine project. Didn't Bobsy tell you yesterday?" Eden turned back to Charly, then looked down at the T-shirt she wore, pointing at the words on it. "That's why there's the petting zoo, the bouncy house, and over there, way in the back, that's where the grime was, the building they tore down and where the new clubhouse, appropriately named Shine—"

"—is going up now, right in front of my eyes," Charly finished for Eden, straining to get a look. "I see. So," Charly said, deciding to make the best of it and not be a baby about it. She'd just have to put the shirt on over her dress. "Let's get to the Shine. I came here to work."

Eden just shook her head. She looked at her feet, then to Charly's. "How? You can't do construction in those shoes, or that dress. Lucky for you, some of us are breaking, so we have time to go find you a pair."

"Charly? Charly, is that you?" a voice yelled, songlike, reminding Charly of one of the Marley brothers. "I was wondering if you were going to show up. You're late, gal!"

Charly closed her eyes, loving the accent. She knew whom the voice belonged to, and just hearing it made the pain she was sure her feet were going to soon suffer worth it. "Faizon! Yes, it's me," she said, smiling and turning around. She admired that he was man enough to wear pink, and thought it looked good against his mocha complexion. She did question his facial hair though. He looked like the caveman in the car insurance commercial. "Yes, me, late and dressed all wrong as you can see. But it's all good."

Faizon sauntered up to her, smiling. He took the baseball hat he wore off his head, then ran his hand over his wild hair that looked like it hadn't been cut in eons. He licked his lips before he spoke again, revealing a small gap between his teeth that she could barely see because of his full mustache and beard. "You? Late? Dressed wrong? Nah, mama. You kidding me? Even if you're running late, you're always on time. Nah'mean? Anyway, we breaking for a half hour, so you're not late. And you can never be dressed wrong." He stuck his hand out, waving it over the actions going on around the huge lot. "If anything, this isn't decorated to suit you, not the other way around." He licked his lips again, looking Charly up and down. "If I'd have known you'd be wearing yellow, I'd have planted more flowers to match your outfit. Yep, yo boy helped finish the fence this morning, and did some of the planting. This area here will be a circular drop-off area where some cars and busses can park. That's why we got two fences up. The ugly orange one will be removed when they lay the cement. I hope you like." He took two steps forward, then wrapped his arms around Charly, rocking her from side to side as if they were old friends or boyfriend and girlfriend. "We're actors, mama. That's why I look like this. I got to get ready for my full facial hair role. That means we can act through anything, even being able to plant. Ya dig? And the fun part of the day is just really getting started. No worries, man. You're here in time for the girls."

Charly laid her head on his shoulder, inhaling his scent. She felt like she was in the middle of a soap opera scene or a fairytale, being saved by Mr. Right or a knight. She almost moaned, fighting with herself to remove her face from the fabric of Faizon's shirt. He smelled nice, and felt even better, which is why she had to disconnect from him. It wasn't that she was wrapped up in him, though he was definitely appealing enough to tempt her to become so. "Let's just hope I can *act* like my feet don't hurt later." She laughed.

"Wow," Faizon said, looking Charly in the eyes after she'd summoned the strength to disconnect from him.

"Careful, mama, that acting thing really works for me. You're going to make a brother feel special and forget professional boundaries," he joked, then smiled.

Charly's lips spread, revealing her teeth. "Well, why would I want to do that?"

"Do what?" Lex asked, walking through the brick pillars and making his way over to them. He had a hammer in his hand and a tool belt around his waist, and he wore a pink shirt too. He stopped, then raked his golden eyes up and down, taking Charly in in one whoosh, nodding in appreciation. "So that's your magic trick to keep your legs tight, huh? You don't just do yoga, like you said. You work out," he began, then turned around and waved the hammer around the lot, indicating the surroundings. He turned back toward her. "Doing construction in stilettos, or whatever they're called—that's athletic in my opinion." He winked. "And I can dig it. It works for you. I can also dig when you've lost a bet. You did, right? You feel better."

Eden cleared her throat. "I have to get Charly some shoes. I don't think Bobsy told her what to wear, Lex."

The twinkle in Lex's golden eyes died. "I didn't bring Bobsy on board to make sure Charly is taken care of, Eden. I got you the gig."

"But Lex, I gave her the itinerary," Eden began. She had a plastered smile on her face, and she looked frazzled and something else Charly couldn't put her finger on. It wasn't fear that registered, and it wasn't embarrassment, but something was definitely looming under the surface.

Charly stepped up, moving toward Lex. She swished her dress as much as she could to get his attention, hoping to break the uncomfortable vibe that was penetrating the air. He wasn't being mean to Eden, but she didn't want Eden to take heat for a minor miscommunication. She had shown her the itinerary, and Charly had asked if they could go over it later, so it wasn't Eden's fault. It was hers. "She's telling the truth, Lex. She gave me the itinerary yesterday morning." She owned her wrongdoing, then turned the tables on him. "Maybe if you hadn't've worked me out so hard, I would've remembered . . . and I wouldn't have overslept from being exhausted and taking your juice. I apologize for being late today," she sang, stabbing him in his granite-hard chest with her index finger. Lex nodded, and his demeanor lightened. "And, if it helps, Bobsy mentioned the project too. I just . . . well, it doesn't matter. I'm here. Let's get to it." She began to walk away, then her heel sank into the dirt. In one second, her fear of crashing was becoming a reality, not because of speeding while riding, but because of speeding while walking. She released her construction hat and T-shirt from her grip, opening her palms to soften her fall.

"Charly! Oh, that is you! Charly! I heard you were coming to help us," a little girl's voice yelled.

Charly picked up her face from the dirty ground, turning it in the direction of the little girl, who she guessed couldn't be more than nine, then her greeted with a smile. The girl had two ponytails and wore a huge snaggle-toothed grin. Her red EMPOWER YOUTH: THE GRIME TO SHINE CREW T-shirt was covered in fresh dirt and paint, and she held a wet paintbrush in one hand and had a bunch of flowers in the other. "Hey! Yes, it's me," Charly said. She widened her smile, then froze at the sight of a group rushing toward them.

Lights flashed. Jean-and-T-shirt-clad reporters, obviously unprofessional and not with a major network, ran toward them from the direction of the street entrance. One of them yelled, "Yep. They're on break!" Without thought or consideration, they all but ran over the little girl with the ponytails.

"Ouch!" the little girl yelled, tumbling over and landing on her side as one of the armed-with-camera novices took it too far.

Charly was on her feet in seconds. She rushed to the little girl's side, pushing the wannabe reporter with all her might. "Get back!" she yelled, reaching for the little girl's hand, but accidentally grabbing the wet paintbrush. Without thought, she wiped the loud red paint on her yellow sundress, and helped the girl to her feet. "What's wrong with you?" she snapped at the guy, walking up on him and shoving him as Lex jumped in front of her, protecting both her and the girl. "Are you okay?" she asked the girl. "You need me to call your mom? Who are you here with?" Maybe she should alert someone in case the little girl was more hurt than she appeared.

The girl nodded. "Yes. I am now!" Her words were as lit as her dazzling eyes. "But I'll be even better if you give me your autograph," she said, then shrugged. "And I'm a big girl. I'm here by myself. I go everywhere by myself because my momma's always at work, and before you ask, I don't have a daddy. . . ." Her words trailed off. "Duck!" she yelled to Charly.

Charly looked behind her and saw one of the reporters' cameras toppling through the air, coming in their direction at top speed. With one swoop of her arm, she reached out to cover the little girl, and tried to make a run for it at the same time. Again, her heel stabbed into the soft dirt and refused to budge. "Ohhh . . ." Her word stretched as the ground zoomed toward her face again, and she met it with a hard thud. The camera landed next to her. She closed her eyes, and heard the curses of Lex and Faizon flinging through the air like objects. "Language! We've got a princess here," she reminded them at the top of her lungs.

As if nothing was occurring, the group advanced, still thrusting microphones and cell phones outward. "Charly! So word is you and Mēkel are secretly dating. So did you catch him cheating on you, or were you sliding out on him? Why was y'all fighting in the shoe store? Lex, do you plan on knocking ol' boy out in the first round? Faizon, are you with Charly now?" various voices questioned them all while Faizon helped Charly up from the ground.

"Block 'em, Lex," Faizon said, then took the little girl's hand. "Go with Eden, lil mama," he directed.

While getting to her feet, Charly saw Lex move forward with his chest thrust out and his arms squared. Security, all wearing red T-shirts, finally swarmed from behind the gates. "Couldn't be, Mēkel's not here," she said, when she thought she spotted a huge man who looked an awful like Butter Pecan, Mēkel's bodyguard.

"Let's get in motion, Charly," Faizon said, pulling her the opposite way of the brick pillars. "The wannabe journalists won't get to us out here. Trust me. There's way too much security."

Charly's brows rose as her feet reluctantly treaded behind Faizon. Running behind the brick-pillared wrought-iron fence would've made more sense to her. With the children and teens in the back, she was certain there would be more than enough safety. "You sure? Wouldn't we be more secure in the event area? I mean with the networks and Lex's staff?"

With his hand holding hers, Faizon led her through the opening of the rugged chain-link fence and onto the sidewalk. "Pardon me, bruh," he said, excusing them past an obvious hardcore thug, who gripped the neck of a beer bottle and was tatted everywhere Charly could see. "Nah, Charly. We're safer here on the streets. Those bootleg journalists don't wanna test these cats out here. Trust." He looked back at her. "And you're in good hands. I may be an actor, but knowing how to get down for mine is real."

9

Faizon hadn't lied; he wasn't window dressing. He was the real thing, and truly held no fear. He had the respect of many of the street guys, Charly discovered as they made their way through the sketchy neighborhood. Boys dressed in the latest trends gave him pounds, thugs nodded their heads in his direction, and even some druggies extended respect to him, telling him how they wanted to be like him when they grew up. Charly took it all in, and relaxed. Yes, she was safe with him, and the rough hood, while it would've been scary to many, wasn't foreign to her. She'd walked through worse on Chicago's South Side, and frequented a bookstore on One-Two-Five in Harlem, a street that outsiders thought was located in a dangerous section of New York, but it wasn't. Not to Charly. She didn't perceive danger the way many did, and this area wasn't too different for her, she noticed as she looked around. Her feet carried her down the cracked, littered sidewalk, and her hand was still in Faizon's as they crossed the intersection. She had no idea where they were going, and really didn't care. With Faizon by her side, she was at ease, and excited to be in his company. Even if it was over one hundred degrees out under the blinding sun, she liked being with him. It wasn't often she got to hang with someone who knew her side of the entertainment business. No, she wasn't on the big screen like him yet, but, like her, Faizon knew what it was like to have to come to life in front of a camera.

"This way, mama," he said, leading her and gripping her hand tighter, assisting her with stepping off the curb and over the grated drain. "You good?" he asked, looking back into her eyes.

Charly squinted, nodding. She held her free hand over her eyes to shield the blinding sunlight and smiled. "Yes. Where are we going?" she asked, scanning her eyes over the area. "Is there a beauty supply or shoe store around here? I really need to grab a pair of flats so I can help."

Faizon took off his baseball hat, then adjusted the clasps on the back of it to her size and put it on her head. "It doesn't really rock with your outfit, but it'll do. I can't have you out here cute and blind, not unless I really do plan on getting it in. 'Cause one of these cats may forget who I am, and try me by hitting on you, nah'mean?" He looked up and down the busy street. "This is the hood, so it has to be at least three beauty supplies around here. You know y'all sisters don't play when it comes to keeping yourselves polished." He laughed.

Charly laughed with him, then laced her arm through his, keeping herself close to him as they approached an oncoming crowd. The group parted as she and Faizon zigzagged their way through, giving their respective hellos and thank-yous to a few who acknowledged them.

"Yo, your last flick was sick," a guy complimented Faizon. "My girl said you shoulda gotten an Oscar for that. Right, baby?" He looked over at a girl to his left, who was pushing a stroller.

Faizon thanked him.

The girl eyed Charly and nodded her hello. "That's a nice purse," she said, then gently shook the stroller handles to rock the baby, who'd begun to whimper. "That's like three months worth of rent, groceries, and diapers. I'll never have nothing like that," she mumbled barely above a whisper, pulling Charly's heart strings. "What you doing around here?" she asked aloud, her expression dull. " 'Cause I know y'all not here to make over anybody's room—not in this neighborhood."

Charly looked the young girl up and down, trying to size her up. She didn't know if the girl was being nasty or honest, but she had Charly's attention. The baby's whimper turned into a cry, and the girl's face held concern. For an instant, Charly wanted to reach out and give her a hug and tell her that everything would be okay, that she could have so much more in life than an expensive designer handbag, but the baby wailed louder, capturing Charly. "You mind?" Charly asked, unleashing her arm from Faizon's, then moving to the front of the stroller. She bent her knees and crouched until she was eye to eye with the cutest little infant she'd seen in a long time. "Is she yours? She's beautiful," she said, almost unable to contain herself. She wanted to reach out and scoop up the baby, who'd stopped crying when Charly spoke. The child was butterball fat and smelled sweet. "She's precious! How old?" Charly looked to the girl, meaning every word.

"She's mine, and she's almost seven months." The girl smiled, and Charly's heart broke for the young mother. She didn't know the girl's situation, but she could guess it was hard to be a teenage parent. The girl had to be younger than her.

Still squatting, Charly reached into the stroller and straightened the baby's dress, then smiled when the baby found her pacifier and stuck it in her mouth. "So what's your name, and why do you think I wouldn't be here to help in this neighborhood?" Charly asked, rising to her feet, and catching sight of plastic grocery bags stored in the stroller's rear basket next to the diaper bag.

The girl shook her head and shrugged. "They call me Charlie, but it's spelled with an 'i-e,' not a 'y' like yours."

Charly's eyes widened, and a smile spread on her face. She'd never met another Charlie before. "Charlie. I love it!"

"But my name is Charlotte. And I don't want to say why you wouldn't be helping here," the girl said.

"Baby, don't get all bashful now. Say what you say when you watch her show," the guy said, nudging her arm.

Faizon moved to Charly's side. Charly raised her brows, waiting. "Well, what do you say?" She tilted her head.

The girl shrugged. "That you only help rich people or teenagers who come from good homes and neighborhoods and schools. Teenagers who have good parents— even if they only have one, that's one more than I have." The girl shook her head. "Y'all never help nobody like us; people who just want to get outta the hood and have a better life." The girl looked down, a mask of defeat covered her face. "Girls like me. I mighta had a baby early, but I took her with me to night classes so I could get my GED."

"And she registered at the community college," the guy added.

Charly's heart dropped. She'd been one of the people the girl spoke about, minus the teenaged mother part, and she remembered it well. She'd wanted to get away from her neighborhood, to capture her dreams, and not live from check to check like her mother. The girl was right. *The Extreme Dream Team* had never remade a teen's room in a neighborhood like the one they were in now or helped a teen who'd had a background close to her own. And Charly knew and would bet a dollar to a dime on it, the way the show was set up—to assist honor roll students, teens with nonprofits and middle- and upper-class do-gooders, the people Americans wanted to see as their future—*The Extreme Dream Team* would probably never help someone like the teen mother who stood in front of her with the beautiful baby. That bothered Charly to the core, but she didn't know what she could do about it.

"I still watch the show though because you're on it. It's cool to see somebody who looks like me star on a reality show. It gives me some hope for her future," she said, nodding toward her baby.

Charly smiled, genuinely touched. "I'll be right back," she said to Faizon. "I'm going to step over there." She pointed a couple of feet away, then beckoned to the young mother. "Can I talk to you in private over there? And please bring the stroller," she said, walking toward the corner store.

"Yeah?" the girl said, catching up to her. "What's up?"

Charly stared into the girl's eyes. "First, I want to thank you. Thank you for watching my show, and thank you for bringing up what you did. And you're absolutely right, I should be helping everyone, especially since I come from a neighborhood like this, and, for a long time, it was pretty much just me and my sister. So I know where you're coming from." She pointed to the stroller. "Pass me one of those grocery bags," she said, fishing out the contents of her purse.

"Why? What are you doing?" the girl asked, reaching in the back of the stroller to get a bag.

"I'm giving you my purse. You said you liked it, so I'm giving it to you," Charly stated, still digging things out of her purse.

"But why?" The girl removed something from the bag, then stood. She handed it to Charly with a smile on her face. "And what are you going to carry? A plastic bag? All day?"

Charly shrugged. "It's not a big deal. I have other purses. I'm giving you this one because I want you to know you can have and be anything you want. I heard you say you'd never have one like this, so now I'm proving you wrong. You can," she said. Then her eyes widened when she looked at the bag the girl was giving her. "Is that what I think it is? A sneaker store bag . . . as in brand-new adult sneakers?"

The girl nodded. "Yeah. You got something against

shoe bags or new tennis shoes or something? And I'm not accepting your purse. I don't do charity. No offense."

Charly looked at the girl's feet, sizing them up. "You have to be at least a size eight, right?" The girl nodded. "I'll tell you what. I can respect you not wanting my charity, though it isn't really charity, so I won't give you my purse. We'll barter. I'll *trade* you my purse for your shoes. I don't even care what they look like, but you have to let me help you help yourself. I want to donate to your education—pay for your college books. If that's not good for you, think of it as a gift for the baby."

"So what's your story, Faizon?" Charly asked, handing him the shopping bag that held the sneakers and, now, the contents of her purse. "I know you're from the islands, but your word choice is very New York. You also have an untouchable demeanor, like you've been seasoned in the streets, but that can't be all. Not with you contributing to this project. So who's the girl that made you want to do this?"

Faizon smiled, nodding. He walked toward the corner, back in the direction of the event. "Let's try there. There's a corner store. They should have some cotton balls to help you fit your too-big sneakers." He laughed, shaking his head. "The things you women come up with. Who woulda thought about putting cotton balls in shoes to make 'em fit?" He reached out, taking Charly's hand in his again. "Okay, mama. So you want my story now? You can't wait for us to have our sit-down after the event?"

Charly shook her head no. "I heard you're only here

for the day, so I need to be sure I get your info. I have to hear it from you because your personality goes into the project. That's the plan, anyway."

He nodded in appreciation. "That's cool, and it's what I want. I guess I should start at the beginning, then bullet-point the main points. I was born in Kingston, Jamaica, to a single mom who moved us to Queens, New York, when I was two. After she scraped her pennies together to feed us while she put herself through school, we moved to Vegas, then to Hollywood. I was around eleven then, which is why I'm a little rough around the edges. I fought in the streets to protect myself in Queens—you'd be surprised how many preteen roughnecks you can encounter," he said, laughing. "Then after we moved to here and to Cali, I had to literally fight my way home from school. My mother was a linguist and vocal coach who helped ac-tors, newscasters, and other TV people lose their accents. So, of course, I can turn mine off and on." He looked at her with pain-filled eyes. "*Was* is the key word, Charly. I lost my mom just a couple months ago to the Big C, as many now call it."

Charly nodded, following him into the market. She didn't know what to say because she knew there were no words to erase his pain. "It's a good thing you're doing, Faizon."

Faizon switched gears, then laughed again. "You know, you're not wrapped too tight, Charly. You could've gotten us robbed or something, pulling out your wallet on the street back there. You must really want to see me act up."

Charly shook her head, looking at her watch. They needed to get back, but she needed the cotton to fit the too-big shoes, and she was thirsty. She exhaled, appreciating the air-conditioning in the store as she found a small cosmetic section and grabbed a bag of puffballs. "You must not know my background," she said to him. "I'm not too much different from you; I'm from both sides of the street too. I can take care of myself and you."

Faizon pulled her in the opposite direction, then walked to the cooler, looking at the contents through the frosty glass. He let go of her hand and laughed. "Word? So you think you can take care of me, huh? Why's that, Charly? 'Cause I've played a dancer, a singer, and have pretty much been typecast for leading male roles in romantic comedies?" He shook his head, sliding open the door. He took out a bottle of water with a blue label, held it up to her. "This brand good for you or do you want another kind?"

Charly shrugged, leaning against the coldness of the cooler's glass. The chilliness climbed her arm, making her tingle. "Water is water."

Faizon nodded. "Yeah. If you say so. But I don't drink nothing else besides what I grew up drinking. I'm not really good with change, and have no desire to become good with it either, unless it's for an acting gig. I can switch back and forth with parts, then I trash the fake to keep myself real. Nah'mean?"

Charly nodded, taking a mental note. His not being adaptable was something she'd have to keep in mind when she came up with the design for the girls' center. She never would've guessed someone as young as Faizon would be so rooted in his ways, but everybody was entitled to their quirks, and she knew from experience, many

artists were eccentric. "Gotcha," she said, surveying the
different brands of water in the cooler, then squatted
down to take one off the bottom shelf.

"Yo! Faizon!" a rough voice growled from behind.

Charly froze and almost swallowed her teeth. She knew
the voice, and would never forget it. Still, she questioned
herself. She'd encountered it almost three-thousand miles
away, so how could the guy be here in Nevada?

"Yo! Faizon! I know that's you with that crazy wild
hair," he growled again, sounding like he could swallow
razor blades and not get cut. His voice was that rugged.

Charly turned slightly, careful not to let the guy see her
face, then looked at Faizon. Faizon nodded at the guy,
squaring his shoulders. "S'up? Of course it's me," Faizon
answered.

From her peripheral, she could see the dude hold up
his open hand, giving Faizon a pound. "Bruh, don't be
s'upping me like that. You betta act like you know a
brutha. I just heard you were getting in today, and I
hoped I'd run into you. I'm out later." He laughed, low
and gruffly. "Good look on the swagger too. I see you're
streeting it up more and more, looking harder and
harder. You almost intimidated me with that crazy hair
and beard. So how long you here for?" he thundered,
then gave a half-smile half-sneer, which died when he
purposely leaned in and looked at Charly. "Yo. I know
you," he said to her. It wasn't a question.

Charly stood, then turned all the way around to face
him. Immediately, she was leery of the guy who met her
eyes, and didn't know how anyone could intimidate him.
She gulped. A huge scar was slashed across one of his

eyes and the brow above it. Another scar ran from the middle of his forehead up to the top of his faded hair. A trio of teardrops was tatted under his eye. She shivered and nodded. He was the motorcycle guy who'd tossed her purse back to her in New York.

Faizon laughed. "Thanks, Coop. I do what I do. It's all in the job, fam. I'm just here for the day. I'm headed back to L.A. tonight on the last flight out. And you gotta stop with the questions. You're gonna scare the lady," he said, nodding toward Charly.

"I wouldn't bet on it—she's not the scared, run-and-call-the-cops type. Right?" Coop asked, eyeing Charly. He turned back to Faizon. "The red-eye, huh? I'm headed to Cali tonight too, on the bus though. Think I can swing a ride with you on your way to the airport?" Faizon nodded. Coop gave him a pound. "So this you, huh?" he said, nodding in approval. He looked back Charly's way. "You that little cutie from that show that helps young knuckleheads?" He nodded, answering his own question. "That's good. Real good stuff you be doing. Guess that's why you hanging out with this dude—he's good too. Pretty much saved my whole fam from being homeless when our crib burned down, and he still refuses to take credit for it. But you know I got long arms, it ain't nowhere I can't reach and nothing I can't find out. Coast to coast." He winked, then reached into his pocket. Charly jumped when he was removing his hand, sure that he had some sort of weapon. He smiled, then handed Faizon and Charly business cards. "Y'all check out my bidness when you get a chance."

"Word? When this happen? Nobody told me," Faizon said, looking down at the card. "This is a'ight, Coop."

Charly looked at the card, and stretched her eyes. Quickly, she reminded herself not to judge someone by his looks. Coop, as Faizon had called him, wasn't all bad. He had, after all, returned her stolen bag. She nodded, then put the card in her wallet inside the plastic shopping bag that now housed all her stuff.

Coop rubbed his stubbly chin, then reached into the cooler and took a bottle of water. He cracked it open, then swigged from the rim. "I just put it together. I figured after the dime I put in, bruh, the least I could do was come out and school some of these young knuckleheads so nobody will lock 'em in a cage for ten years too. They treat you just like an animal in there, bruh. And these knuckleheads need to know they ain't nobody's animal, and it's up to me to school 'em." He averted his attention to Charly. "Everybody deserves a second chance, right?" He shrugged. "Sometimes the knuckleheads do stupid stuff, and end up getting locked up. Other times, I'm able to step in and save 'em. I try to clean up their mess, then I teach them how not to make a mess." He finished off the water bottle, then looked back at Faizon. "Yeah, man, after what you all are doing for girls, I figured I could do the same for boys. But we ain't gone be rocking pink though. No disrespect." He laughed.

Faizon reached over and gave Coop a brotherly hug. "That's cool, Coop. Let me know if there's anything I can do. You know, we're kinda busy now with the girls' project, but you know how it goes."

Coop reached into his jeans pocket and took out a ring of keys. He wiggled them in the air. "My house keys." He nodded. "Yeah, bruh, because of you, I do know how it goes. I know you helped my fam. So let me know if there's anything I can do."

Faizon nodded. "Yes, there's one thing. Charly here was getting attacked by some bootleg Internet journalists down behind the gate. You know the one with the bright orange strips in it, the same one we're going to tear down after the girls' center goes up? The only people who should be back there will be rocking shirts like mine, but in pink, red, or white. The shirts are considered their passes. Can you—"

"I gotchu, fam. We on it. 'Sides, the last time I heard ain't no bootleg journalist requested permission to be in my neighborhood." He laughed, then looked at Charly. "You keep doing good, cutie. You got our support. And who knows, maybe one day your show can look out for us here. I may not be a school academic, but I'm a street scholar schooling my people to keep them outta jail. Somebody gotta give them an opportunity because the world—sometimes even their mommas—won't."

Charly smiled, a little confused. She wouldn't have pegged Faizon to be one to request help to keep her protected, but decided not to question it. Maybe he was aware of more danger than she knew of, which made her feel more at ease with Coop. The guy was really trying to help youth, and she couldn't help but respect it, even if he did look like someone from a horror flick. "I'll keep that in mind. And like Faizon, if I can do anything to help, I will. The world didn't give me a chance either. I took it."

"Word! I like that. Faizon, you gotchu a live one there!" Coop winked at Charly, but it wasn't sign of disrespect or interest. It was full of admiration. "Okay, Ms. Take It, remember if there's anything you need, you come see me. I'll take care of you. I *owe* you that," Coop said, and Charly knew he meant it.

10

Children's laughter sounded over music, the scent of barbecue wafted through the air, and white-, red-, and pink-shirted people—the invitees, crew members, and the team, respectively—moved about the area when Charly and Faizon returned. Charly nodded, noting that Bobsy had predicted correctly. News crews and reporters were scattered throughout the crowd. She hoped that Coop and his people wouldn't give them a hard time, and could distinguish the professionals from the novices.

She parted from Faizon, who was on his way to help on the other side of the event, while she went to lend her expertise to the other. She smiled, approaching a group of teen girls who were working with the guys on the projects. Some were assigned to Shine, the Las Vegas retreat; others were ambassadors of some of the other retreats that Charly hoped to help design. She waved to the girls, trying to stay upbeat, but it was hard after she'd gotten close enough to see them. Many wore headscarves or construction hats, and others were comfortable enough to show their heads that were either bald or close to it. A few girls were in wheelchairs, while some others—well, Charly didn't know what was going on with them, but they didn't look healthy. All seemed happy, though.

"Hi, Charly!" one girl called out, running over to meet her. "I'm Destiny." She tipped her construction hat, revealing a bald head underneath. She rubbed her hand over her scalp, then stuck out her tongue. "You like my 'do?" Destiny asked, smiling, without the least bit of self-pity.

Charly tilted her head, returning the smile and admiring the girl. Destiny was brave and beautiful. "I do like your 'do," she said, thinking how Destiny's lack of hair made her pretty face really stand out. "It's a lot cooler than mine. Pun intended." Charly felt safe to tell her joke, especially when Destiny laughed.

Destiny nodded. "Eden was right. She said we'd like you. It's nice to meet people who don't feel *too* sorry for us. And you're right twice; I can feel a breeze much better than you." She ran a dainty hand over her head, pretending to push back long locks.

"Too sorry?" Charly questioned, wrapping one arm around Destiny and walking back toward the group.

Destiny side-eyed her. "Yes. Too sorry. We don't want you to feel too sorry for us because then you pity us and make us feel bad for ourselves. And self-pity is not cool when you're fighting for your life. But feeling a little sorry for us is okay because then we get great gifts like these retreats and scholarships, and we get to hang out with celebrities." Destiny cracked up laughing, and Charly joined her. "Those are things I never would've dreamed of before, ya know, and I was valedictorian and from low-income housing," she pointed out, refraining from naming her illness. "Oh, Eden left you a hat and T-shirt over there." She pointed to a nearby table.

Charly's eyebrows rose. It was like every other turn she made, a girl was mimicking a part of her story, and feeding her desire to help girls who hailed from situations like hers—poor and almost parentless, which she would've been had she not found her dad. No, Charly hadn't been and would never be valedictorian; she was a proud C+, bordering on B-, student, but her sister, Stormy, was the smartest person in her class every time, and not once had anyone saved them from their dismal life because of Stormy's grades. "Destiny, introduce me to the other girls. I want to really get to know all of you, and not just your diagnosis because, as you know, you are not your illness," she said, walking to the table. She put on the construction hat, grabbed a hammer, and remembered how she used to assure herself that she wasn't a product of her situation, she was the way out of it.

Charly stood with her palm shielding her eyes from the sun that the construction hat couldn't block, looking at the community center. The rooms inside had been framed, and she and the girls had helped with some dry-walling and painting. Now they were prepping to put color palettes together with décor and vote on little touches that would make the center truly theirs. Faizon jogged by

Charly, waving. Charly waved back, laughing. He and Lex had checked on her progress several times since she'd begun working, and had playfully accused her and the girls of outdoing their contributions. She admired how he and Lex took the event so seriously, yet still managed to have a good time with the girls.

"Have fun!" she yelled, then looked down at the clipboard in her hand. Something was missing—a splash of brightness was needed for the library, something vivid that would offset the dull earth tones. "Hmm." She tried to think of a color besides pink. It wasn't that she was against it; she just didn't want the girls who were fighting cancer to always have to be surrounded by walls that looked like they'd been dipped in Pepto Bismol.

"Charly! Charly!" Lex's deep voice called out.

Charly looked up, then stood on tiptoe, turning her head in the direction of his voice. She cupped a hand on the side of her mouth, then shouted: "Girls rule, Lex. You've got strength, but girls are stronger!"

Her crew, as she'd begun to call the girls, clapped and cheered, then chanted: "Girls are stronger! Girls are stronger!"

"Yes! We are!" Charly said, then snapped her fingers. "Come over here, and tell me what you guys think of this color for the library wall," she said, walking back over to a picnic table and looking at paint swatches. "I'm thinking a deep majestic purple, bordering on a midnight navy-bluish. Something kinda dark, but not dreary—"

"Charly! Charly!" a different male voice called her name. It wasn't deep like Lex's. It didn't sound anything remotely close to Faizon's, and since it was a guy's, she knew it didn't belong to Eden.

Charly stepped away from the picnic table to see whom the voice belonged to, and saw a blur of red whiz past her, followed by a few more blurs of crimson. "Take this," she said to Destiny, then handed over the clipboard. "You take the lead, and I'll be right back. Maybe you guys can vote on the color before then," she encouraged, walking toward the guy in red, who was still calling her name, and was now jumping up and down. "Yes. I'm right here," she stated.

"Charly! You've got to go." His whisper came out more like a loud, breathy scream. "It's important!"

Charly tilted her head and hit him with a barrage of questions. "Why are you screaming and whispering? What do you mean, I've got to go? What's up? What happened? Is it an emergency?"

He was still moving a lot, and his eyes were stretched. His expression was one of panic, and he was clearly upset. He grabbed her wrist. "C'mon, Charly. You've gotta hurry up before the rest of the team leaves. There's a situation at Lex's."

Charly held up her hand. "Wait. Wait. Slow down. What do you mean before the rest of the team leaves? I just saw Faizon and Lex—"

He cut her off. "Getting ready to leave. Faizon and Lex were leaving. That's why they were calling you."

"Wait here!" Charly said, then turned around and ran back to the girls. She told them she'd return as soon as possible, and lied, assuring them that she was just running out to get needed supplies. Out of breath, she made

it back to the crew member. "Okay. I'm ready. So I'm riding with Eden, I guess. Since everyone else is gone."

The guy shook his head, grabbing her wrist and leading her toward the gate. "No. Eden's gone. You'll have to
go with Mēkel. He just got here."

11

They had only been feet apart for a matter of seconds, and Charly's stomach was already starting to churn. Mēkel, her arch nemesis, was half standing, half leaning on the hood of a luxury convertible car. His arms were defensively crossed, and his long legs were stretched out in front of him. The dimple in his left cheek was deeper than she'd remembered, reminding her of a bowl of hot fudge. He was a tall, rich, and delicious dessert—good in small doses, but too much of him couldn't be healthy. Not if a girl didn't want to fall for him, Charly thought, fighting an urge to smile, which only confirmed his natural ability to attract. She couldn't stand him, yet, here she was battling herself not to be nice. She blamed it on his natural swagger, which commanded respect, and his bigger-than-life presence, which was only rivaled by his gorgeousness. He was obscenely cute. Charly put on her sunglasses and shook her head. It made no sense for a guy to be so tempting, and she was glad that she didn't have to be in his company on a regular basis.

"Are you just going to stand there? Or are you coming?" he asked, making Charly stare at his mouth. He had the most perfectly even, straight, gleaming white teeth she'd ever seen, and every time he spoke, he looked as if he were about to smile. But she knew better. His serious tone and ambiguous expression told her he wasn't overcome by glee. Still, his dimple deepened and danced with each syllable he uttered.

Charly blinked behind the sunglasses, glad that he couldn't see her eyes. She didn't like that she couldn't read him. She expected him to spit on the ground, call her a name, say or do something that would give away his feelings. But he didn't. He was just as cool and calm as he'd been in the sneaker store, and she wondered if he possessed feeling at all. The way he just stood there, staring into her soul without blinking, caused her uneasiness. "I'm not happy about riding with you either, Mēkel," Charly answered, then wished she would've thought before she spoke. "And can't you close the top on this car? I've been baking in this sun all day."

Mēkel walked to the driver's side. He got in the car without reply, making her feel small from lack of recognition. He glanced sideways when she got in next to him, then quickly turned his attention back toward the street. He put on his seat belt, started the car, and revved the engine, while he drummed on the steering wheel and bounced to a song that must've been playing inside his head. He also ignored her request to close the top.

For seconds, Charly watched him move his neck back

and forth like a gobbling turkey to a beat she couldn't hear. She grew tired of waiting for the song that played in his head to end. She cleared her throat as loud as she could, trying to interrupt him, but he didn't budge. "Well? Are you going to keep bobbing your head like you're in the studio? Or are we going to ride to whatever this emergency is?" she snapped, then looked up. She took off her sunglasses. The sky had quickly gone from vibrant to dull as the clouds moved in front of the sun.

Mēkel held up his thumb in the air, wagging it in her direction. "You're not in."

"What?" Charly asked, redirecting her eyes at him and throwing up her palms, frustrated. "I am in! Let's go."

He really looked at her then. "Do you always have to be so disagreeable, Charly?" he asked coolly. "Being bossy doesn't make you a boss; being in control does. You need to learn control." He unfastened his seat belt, then moved toward her.

"What are you doing?" Charly asked, sucking in her already flat stomach and tried to meld with the seat as Mēkel reached one long arm across her. He grabbed the passenger seat belt and tried to slide it across her midsection, but it kept locking in place. While he pulled, released it, then tugged on it again, she held her breath to prevent herself from inhaling whatever scent he wore. It wasn't that he didn't smell good, because he did. It was that she didn't want his essence lingering in her memory like his songs remained in her mind. A loud click, and it was over. He was back in his seat again, fastening in, and she began breathing.

"Which way?" he asked, moving the car's gearshift to

DRIVE, and putting on his own pair of shades as the sun reappeared.

Charly shook her head in disbelief, and put back on her sunglasses. How could he not know where they were going? "You mean you don't know how to get there?"

The way he turned his face toward her answered for him. He put the car back in park, hopped out, then disappeared through the gates. Charly dug in the shopping bag that held the contents of her purse and the high heels she'd worn earlier. She took out her phone, deciding to call Eden, then rolled her eyes. She hadn't programmed Eden's info into her cell. "Or Lex's or Faizon's," she was chastising herself, when the driver's door opened.

Mēkel slid back into the seat with his cell phone in his hand. He scrolled to something, touched the screen, and put it to his ear. "No one. I can't get in touch with anyone. Can't get a single person on the line, and all I remember are three numbers: mine, my sister's, and my mother's. I just upgraded my phone yesterday, and I didn't have time to transfer my contacts," he said, then ended the call. He rubbed his palms over his face. Charly assumed that was a sign of frustration for him, but she couldn't be sure because he still seemed emotionless. He looked at Charly. "Nobody's back there who can direct us, and the others don't know Lex's new address." His hands were on the steering wheel again, but there was no drumming. He shook his head, then shrugged. "I don't know how everybody disappeared. It makes no sense." He was still shaking his head when he went through his day. "I got here. They were running out. Some kind of emergency. 'Wait for Charly. She knows how to get there,' " he said. He looked at her. "That's what Whip said. He said you knew how to get to Lex's."

Charly nodded. "I was paying attention. Street names, landmarks . . . I can get us back. Make a U-turn," she said, sure of the direction. "Then at the second light, take a left, then turn at the first right. Go straight until I tell you when."

The car pulled off slowly, then crawled down the street. Mēkel turned up the music, and his beautiful voice belted through the speakers. The melody was fantastic, but the artist was a piece of work, and not a good one, she decided, losing patience. Mēkel drove like he was afraid of the speed limit, and their moving like a turtle was irritating her. What was the point of driving a car that could reach race-car speeds if you were afraid to open up the engine?

"Did you say we were driving to an emergency or in a funeral procession?" she asked. "Because you drive slower than I can walk."

His phone rang.

Her phone rang.

The sun disappeared again.

They both looked into their laps.

Charly's screen read UNKNOWN. "I don't take blocked calls, but considering the circumstances . . . ," she said, thinking it better for her to be on a call than him, since he was driving and seemed to be struggling with that. "Hello," she answered, looking at him.

"My call's coming up blocked too. No surprise, all of us program our phones to block our numbers," Mēkel explained, then touched the screen on the dash. "Hello?" he said aloud, then shot her a look. He winked. "Blue-tooth," he mouthed.

"Hurry up, yo! Something's seriously wrong..." Faizon's voice boomed through the speakers, then faded into a deafening silence.

Eden was in Charly's ear, but Charly couldn't hear her say anything other than "emergency" before her phone went silent too. She looked at the screen to see if they were still connected, and noticed she had just 10 percent of her battery juice left. She shook her head, looking at Mēkel. "We gotta go, Mēkel. You're driving too slow."

Mēkel looked at her, and she could see discomfort on his face. He pointed ahead, then put his hand back on the steering wheel. He gripped it until the color drained from his knuckles, then swerved the car into the next lane. "I need to get over and find another main road. There's an accident ahead. Look. I couldn't drive fast if I wanted to."

His phone rang again, quieting their conversation. Charly reached forward and touched the dashboard screen where he had, but it didn't work. She pressed again and again, in several places until she heard the ringing cease and background noise filter in through the stereo speakers. "Hello," she answered. "Faizon?"

"No, it's Lex, Charly. Where's M ..." The silence returned.

"Lex. Lex! I'm here. Can you hear me? Because I can't hear you. We need an address," Mēkel shouted as if speaking loud would secure the connection.

"... two, zero ..." Silence. "... Place. You got it?" Silence. "Bobsy, bruh . . ." More silence. A triple chime replaced Lex's voice, telling them the call had dropped on Lex's end. The doo-doo-dooo kept playing over and over.

"Uh, that dinging is irritating," Charly said. She touched the screen to disconnect, but was unsuccessful. She continued to touch until it worked.

"System Locked," a computerized voice said from the speakers.

Charly glanced at Mēkel. "Sorry," she said, then felt bad for him. She had never seen all the color drain from a chocolate-coated-looking brother's face before, but now she knew it was possible. Mēkel had gone from delicious cocoa-brown to dull oatmeal in a matter of seconds. He'd also transformed into a race-car driver, she noticed when he hit the accelerator and zipped from one lane to the next, to another, then screeched to a stop.

He banged the steering wheel, and she no longer had to question if he was capable of having emotions or not. At that moment, he was clearly wrapped in his feelings. He shook his head. "Not good . . ."

"I know. This is awful," Charly said. She looked at him, pressing her lips together. "Call your mother or sister. Maybe one of them can three-way Lex or Faizon . . ." She snapped her fingers. "Your attorney. You and Lex and Faizon share an attorney, so your mother or sister can call him, and he can give us the numbers." She nodded, pleased with her solution. "And I wonder what's happened to Bobsy. It must've just happened, whatever it is, because Bobsy seemed okay earlier, and was intent on doing whatever it is that trainers do."

Mēkel looked at her. "My mother's out of the country,

and I can't call my sister. Obviously." Charly just looked at him, wondering what was so obvious. "And Bobsy's not a trainer," he continued.

Charly laughed a little. Clearly Mēkel had been missing for a while like Eden had said he had a habit of doing while he was recording. "I was just with Bobsy, and you don't know what you're talking about. He is too a trainer."

Mēkel shook his head at Charly. "No. Bobsy. Is. Not. A. Trainer. Charly," he said slowly and deliberately, then whipped the nose of the convertible between two cars, and barely missed crashing into one of them. At no less than sixty miles an hour, he'd taken the corner, and the wheels squealed. He was cutting it too close for Charly's comfort. He banged angrily on the steering wheel. "And this you can't fight me on. Bobsy is not a trainer. Bobsy isn't a he either, she's a she. And *she* is my sister. My very ill sister, who obviously can't answer her phone because there's an emergency." His normally too-cool voice cracked.

Charly's eyes stretched. She had been wrong. Mēkel did have feelings, and was obviously hurting. And now she understood why Bobsy hated her guts. She knew she wouldn't be too pleased if someone kept referring to her as a boy. "Bobsy is your *sister?*"

He nodded, and held up a two-fingered peace sign. "Yep. It's just us three—me, my mom, and Bobsy." He continued to drive distracted.

"Pull over. Pull over!" Charly yelled at Mēkel, who was playing a game of accelerate, stop, accelerate, stop. He was pressing the gas pedal, zipping for a half a block at top speed, before punching the brakes, making them skid to a halt as the traffic continued to crawl. "Pull over and let me drive, Mēkel. I remember Whip's shortcut," she said, recalling street names and the landmarks, and how she'd once loved something about the guy sitting next to her, like his voice, and still loved some of those things. His desire to help the less fortunate was one of them. His being a gentleman, who'd tried to come to her rescue, was another. She couldn't tell him that though, just as she couldn't admit she hadn't known about the project when they'd had it out in the store. That would be like committing career suicide, and would also get Mr. Day in trouble for lying to cover her. She could, however, ease some of Mēkel's stress by driving for him while he thought, she decided, looking at him. She had to find some way to get into his good graces as Mr. Day had suggested. She had to stop him from wanting to find a loophole and, thus, a way out of the contract. The girls needed the facility. Charly needed it too.

12

"I hope you got bail money!" Charly yelled over the whoosh of wind that seemed to blow out of nowhere. Seconds ago, the air had been still, but now it breezed angrily. She looked both ways, searching for police and oncoming traffic, then whipped a U-turn, making the back end of the convertible slide, then straighten as she punched the accelerator. They rocketed down the main road as she searched for a recognizable street sign. No, she hadn't memorized them all, but she knew she'd remember the names when she saw them. At least, that's what she was banking on. "There!" she shouted. "We make a right at that stop sign." She skidded to a halt at the four-way stop, looked both ways just in case there were any other drivers on the road who were driving like her, then floored the accelerator again as she hung a sharp right. Her heart raced as fast as the car, and her adrenaline escalated faster. "I can't get stopped by the police. . . ."

She glanced at Mēkel, who held on tight. He seemed unfazed from the waist up, but his feet told a different story. "You know, this isn't a driver's-ed car. There are no brakes on the passenger side. So why do you keep pressing invisible pedals? Am I scaring you?" she asked, laughing. She wanted to lighten the mood.

Mēkel just nodded. "Do you know where you're going? Really? Or are you just winging it?" he asked as she hung another right, then made a U-turn, which indicated she had gone the wrong way.

The sky rumbled above them, and the wind became violent. It was completely charcoal gray out now, and getting bleaker by the second. Charly made another turn, and knew exactly where they were. They were on the street where the police had stopped her and Whip. That meant they only had a couple more blocks before they reached the shortcut. "I gotcha, Mēkel. Don't worry. I'll get you to Bobsy really soon." She floored the pedal, whipping the car through the neighborhood back streets, and then made her way onto the road she'd been looking for. "Hold on!" she yelled at Mēkel, then drove the car as fast as it would go.

"Wait!" Mēkel yelled. "Don't you see that?" He pointed in front of them. "This street runs out. And you're going too fast. You're going to kill us!" He was pressing his foot on the floor again, searching for an invisible brake pedal. "Char-lee!" his sung her name as the car literally took flight, and soared through the air for a second. It'd jumped the pavement, then bounced on the sand. "Stop the car! Stop the car! Now!"

But Charly couldn't stop. She distinctly remembered

Whip saying that staying in motion was the key to not getting stuck in the sand. She shook her head in the negative. "Can't do it," she screamed over the now howling wind. Lightning struck in the distance. "The top, Mēkel. Close the top!" she urged. "It's getting ready to rain."

"Can't," Mēkel said through clenched teeth. "I think we have to be in park or something. Even if we didn't, we wouldn't be able to close the top, not with you driving so fast." He steadied himself by pressing his palms against the dashboard. "Turn on the lights. It's getting dark."

"Bull if we can't close the top," Charly said, locating a button on the left side of the steering wheel that brought the lights to life. She turned the car, heading toward a street that would take them to another set of back roads. That was her plan, anyway, but she couldn't be sure. She had to trust her gut to guide them because there was nothing paved in sight. It was just her and Mēkel, the car, and the desert. Assured that they couldn't crash because there was nothing to run into, Charly pressed her index finger on the touch screen, hoping that the home screen would appear and that a digital button would show so she could close the convertible top.

"System locked," the car said.

Lightning danced again in the sky.

"No way." Charly touched the screen again. And again. And again. With each touch, her fingers pressed harder.

"System locked," the car repeated.

"Unlock it," she said to Mēkel just as thunder rumbled.

"Can't," he informed her, now holding on to the door handle. "Charly! Watch out!"

Charly looked ahead of them, and her eyes widened. Either the darkening sky or the headlights had to be affecting her vision. "That can't be a cliff, can it? Not in the desert, right?" She jammed her foot on the brake, but the car kept moving. The wheels had locked, but the convertible slid across and down the sand like marbles rolling down a wet glass slope, finally stopping in a deep hollow of desert. Charly banged the wheel. "You've got to be kidding me!"

Mēkel looked at her, shaking his head. "No, Charly. You've got to be kidding me!"

She shrugged. "Sorry?" Her apology came out more like a question. "But I still know which way to go, so we're good. It may take us longer because we'll have to walk, but it can't get worse. Right?" she assured.

The sky opened up. Lightning danced, thunder boomed, and large, teardrop-sized raindrops poured from above.

"Can't get worse, huh?" Mēkel asked, trying to open the door, but it barely moved. With rain drenching him, he pushed himself up and made his way over the side of the car. He walked around the vehicle, and put his hands on the sides of his head. "Can't get any worse?! The front of the car is smashed, Charly. This isn't my car—it's a rental, and I'm the only driver covered under the insurance! I'm going to be hit for like a hundred thousand and change!"

A hundred thousand? "Bobsy, Mēkel—Bobsy. We've got to focus on Bobsy," Charly said, trying to sway his attention, and hers, for that matter. She couldn't even fathom a hundred-thousand-dollar charge for a rental car, let alone think about buying one that cost so much. "Think about your sister," she reminded him, climbing out.

Mēkel nodded, his cool demeanor returning. "You're right. I'll think about my sister. You think about how you're going to pay for the car you just wrecked—and not in installments either."

Her best friend, Lola, would think that this was amazing, but Charly considered it a nightmare. Here she was, walking in the rain with one of the hottest guys on earth, with nothing accompanying them but hazy dark clouds and sand under their feet. If they had been on a beach on the coast of some exotic island, it would have seemed romantic, but it wasn't. It was a disaster, and it was her fault. With her plastic shopping bag in her hand bouncing against her leg with each step, Charly pressed onward against the heavy rain, walking in the direction of what she hoped was the street. Still, she couldn't be sure, but she couldn't tell Mēkel that. He was too upset, and not just about the car. He had a serious case of Bobsy on the brain, and kept checking his phone.

He shook his head, stopped in his tracks, and drew back his arm like a quarterback. His stance and guttural groan told her that he'd planned on chucking the cell, which was still in his hand, across the dark desert. Suddenly, he dropped his arm to his side. "Still no signal! But what else can you expect in the middle of the desert?" he snapped. "Control," he said to himself. "Maintain control."

"Why do you keep saying that?" Charly asked, shielding her eyes from the storm. She turned around completely to face him, and her long wet hair whipped across her eyes and the shopping bag swished back and forth, making wet crunching noises. "Ouch!" she said, wiping them as if she could erase the sting with her palms. "That's it," she stated, fed up with her drenched 'do that had become a sponge for the downpour and a spout for the water that kept cascading down her face. She pulled off her now dark pink T-shirt, wrung it out, then wrapped it around her head, twisting and tucking it until she looked Erika Badu-ish. She nodded, glad for the reprieve. It was heavy, but it stopped the raindrops from blurring her vision. "So why?"

Mēkel caught up to her, then looked down at the shopping bag. He met her eyes again. "Why not? If it keeps me calm, if it stops me from *letting* a situation control me instead of me controlling the situation, why wouldn't I remind myself to stay in control? I master myself by allowing or not allowing things to get to me."

Charly shrugged. He could say whatever he wanted about self-mastery, but she knew better. "You can't control everything, ya know?" She waved her hand across the bleakness. "Like this. You can't stop the rain. You can't stop us from being stuck out here. You can't run the whole show by looking for loopholes to get out of the show. That's not being a boss; that's being bossy. Out of control, remember? Your words," she finished, remembering he wanted out of the project because they'd clashed in the sneaker store.

Mēkel's hand was on her shoulder, turning her around. "You're wrong. Self-centered—which is way worse than selfish, by the way—and wrong. I can control many things. Maybe not the rain or being stuck, but I can control how I react. As a professional and a man, I should always maintain some type of control, which is more than I can say for you. You can't and don't try to control anything, not positively. Unless it has something to do with your career and the spotlight—then you're up for anything. That's why you jumped on the opportunity to help with the project, because our centers will give you enough press for your own show." The wind whipped angrily again, making the plastic shopping bag swirl. Mēkel looked at it. "And why are you carrying that stupid shopping bag around?"

Charly's neck almost snapped off, she'd reared it back so hard and quick. "Excuse? For your information, I was already working on my pilot, and the last time I checked, you're working on a new album . . . which will be released at the same time the show will air. Coinkydink? I think not!" She crossed her arms. "Yes, it's a business opportunity, just like it is for you three, but it's also personal for me. Check my résumé, I'm known for helping. And you're known for running off and crying like a baby for an attorney to get you out of a project because you can't see eye to eye with me!" She turned and marched off with the bag bouncing off her leg.

Mēkel jogged behind her. "You must be joking. I'm not a baby—I'm a brother and a boss. The brother who listened to Bobsy, who thought you'd be great for the show, and the boss who came up with the idea for it."

"Yes, and it was you who ran to the attorneys to get out of it! And you talk about control. Puhleez! If anything, you're letting me control you. You want to walk on a huge project—a project to help people who were put in a position they didn't ask for—because you clashed with me." She turned around and faced him, looking him dead in the eyes. "So that means I'm bigger and badder than your desire to help. Okay, so I flipped on you. So what! I was being attacked, Mēkel, and I reacted. Who wouldn't have? I didn't know you were pulling me away from the madness. I thought you were a part of the madness. Remember, all I could see and feel was your hand pulling me. And because I come from a place I didn't ask to be in—a position not too different from the girls, except mine was battling to get out of a bad situation, not for my life—I'm a fighter." She laughed, but it wasn't funny. "I'm a fighter, and you're a fleer. That's what they say people do when faced with something scary, right, fight or flight? Well, you're definitely the scared, go-running-home type." She turned and walked.

He ran in front of her and stopped. His eyes shot daggers into hers. "I'm not afraid of nothing, Charly. And I don't run. I avoid trouble. It's not the same thing. And you want to know how much of a fighter I am? Let me tell you, it was me who fought—fought hard—for you to work on the project. No one else wanted a girl. It was supposed to be an all-guy project, meaning bringing on your boyfriend, Liam, not you—and then you had the nerve to turn on me. Me!" he said, pounding his chest. "Me, who technically hired you, when I was trying to save you in the store! And to make it worse, even after you saw it was me, you still didn't apologize, and you knew I had contracted with the show to get you on board. You knew at least a week before the incident."

Charly's jaw dropped, and she had no words. What could she possibly say? "Sorry" wasn't enough. "I didn't know" wasn't possible. Like a coward, she shrugged. "Thank you . . . ?" It was a try, she told herself. After all, she hadn't thanked Mēkel for helping her in the store or for waiting around while everyone else rushed off to the emergency.

"Thank me? You want to thank me, Charly? Get us out of here!" Mēkel yelled, then walked off, obviously forgetting his control mantra. He turned slightly. "And oh, yeah. Besides doing something with that dreadful bag that keeps rattling, you may want to do something about your clothes. I can see your breasts and panties and legs through your dress."

Charly looked down, and sure enough, Mēkel was right. She looked like she'd been in a wet T-shirt contest; her thin yellow summer dress didn't hide anything. With the drenched fabric, she looked completely naked from the ankles up. She put her head in her hands, hiding the embarrassment.

"Here," Mēkel said, startling her. She looked up, and there he was back in front of her, shirtless. He held out the shirt he had worn. "You can wear this. It's like three times your size, so it should cover all your goodies. Let's go find a way out of here, or at least walk until I can pick up a signal and dial 911 or something."

Charly nodded, slipping into his shirt and a new outlook on Mēkel. With just one outburst and a single article of clothing, Mēkel had changed her mind about him. He was a gentleman and very mature. He'd fought for her to work on their project, and had protected her in the store. She blinked quickly, and not because of the pelting raindrops. She rapidly batted her eyelids in disbelief at what she was seeing and feeling. Mēkel walked in front of her, shirtless and fabulous. *Oh, God. Did I just fall for my nemesis?* "There! Over there!" Charly shouted, a lot more loudly than she'd planned.

Mēkel looked to the right. "Okay. A water tower. Now what?" He held up his phone, which chimed. His eyes stretched as he looked at the screen. "We need to hurry up, Charly. Lex texted me. They're at the hospital." He looked at her. "So the water tower," he repeated. "Now what?"

Charly's anxiety rose. It would be up to her to get them to Bobsy. She pressed her lips together in thought. "Look out for a skyscraper."

Mēkel's laugh wasn't joyful; it was one of disbelief, laced with panic. "The strip is full of those. They're called casinos."

Charly shook her head. "No. Never mind, just follow me." She looked around, then saw her landmark. Just up ahead, there was a skyscraper that appeared to be next to the water tower. Charly smiled. Finally, she knew where she was. "I saw those when I rode through here earlier with Whip. They were on the right, so as long as we walk ahead, keeping them on our left, we should make it to the street."

13

They hopped out of the taxi they'd managed to secure after making their way to civilization and walked into the hospital looking like two cave dwellers. His jeans were dirty and torn, revealing his boxer shorts, which she hadn't noticed before, and he was still shirtless. On his feet was a pair of once-white sneakers that were now a soggy gray, and audibly sloshed with each step. Charly still had the pink shirt wrapped around her head, and not neatly, she noticed, seeing her reflection in the glass. It was tilted to the side in a haphazard mess, and clashed with Mēkel's T-shirt that hung on her like a blood-red mini dress. "Awful," she said, looking at his shirt that was atop her sand-covered yellow halter dress, which now bordered on a nude-ish tan due to her complexion showing through. She looked at her feet, and didn't even want to think about the brown sneakers she wore.

"Stairs," he ordered, walking quickly. "This way."

Charly followed suit, trying to keep the shopping bag still and noting that Mēkel knew the way without direction from a hospital employee. He'd been through this before, she realized, and she wondered how many times. *How long has Bobsy been sick?* She raced to keep up with him as he pushed through one door, then quickly walked to another, then through a corridor, and finally stopped in front of a door that read EXIT. The bag swooshed again, making crumpling noises this time. "Sorry," she apologized for the noise. He pushed it open, then held it for Charly, who rushed through it, then stopped and looked at him. "But why is Bobsy here? Shouldn't she be with you or your mom in Cali or wherever?"

Mēkel shook his head. "Bobsy's doctor moved here. He's the best, and I'm too busy recording and touring, and my mom country hops because she thinks there's some natural cure somewhere else. America isn't big on natural cures, if you haven't noticed. And Lex's pops . . . well, he's like our extended/adopted family, and he's into all natural too, and he insisted Bobsy stay at the camp, where she can have the twenty-four-hour supervision we can't give." He looked at the bag. "You still didn't say why you're carrying that bag around." He pointed at the steps. "Four flights, and then a bridge," he said, then raced around her and bounded up the stairs with Charly in tow, as she followed, explaining why she was carrying a plastic bag.

They were entering the hospital wing before she knew it. An antiseptic smell assaulted her nostrils and bright fluorescent lights blinded her. She strode quickly behind

Mēkel, following him through another exit and across a long corridor, which ended in another door. They pushed through it, and, for a second, she stopped. Everything around her had changed. There was no sickly smell permeating the air, no tile floors, no hospital feeling. It was if they'd entered some swanky hotel. "Where are we?"

Mēkel looked behind him. "Private quarters."

Charly paused. For Bobsy to be here, she had to be very sick. Like gravely ill. "Oh, no . . ."

Mēkel shook his head. "Not that bad. It's just a perk that, fortunately, money can buy." He kept walking, nodding at some employees. Then he slowed, and Charly's eyes widened as they approached a group of guys.

"Everybody's here," she said, then wanted to kick herself for stating the obvious. Lex, Faizon, and Whip stood against one wall, and Eden paced in front of them. Her arms were crossed, and her face seemed to have aged from worry. Charly took it all in, but was stumped by the other visitor, whom she hadn't expected to see. "Coop? Right? What's he doing here?" she asked.

Mēkel glanced over his shoulder, and kept walking. "Cooper," he said with disgust. "That effin' Lex and Faizon," he mumbled. "He would show now . . . as if he's cared." He mumbled something unintelligible under his breath again, but Charly could make out bits and pieces of what sounded like "Cooper is the oldest."

Charly's jaw hit the floor again. She was certain she'd misheard Mēkel. "Did you just say he's the oldest? The oldest as in how? Like your big brother? I thought you said it's just you, your mom, and Bobsy."

Mēkel stopped and turned. His palms were on his face

again, a sign she'd recognized earlier as his way of showing stress. She saw him move his lips, mouthing, *Control . . . control.*

"I did say that. It is—has been only me, my mother, and Bobsy, until recently. Technically, Cooper is the first child my mother gave birth to, but that doesn't make him me or Bobsy's big anything. He's never been big on anything except throwing his genius away and getting into trouble and spending my mother's savings on criminal lawyers."

Charly's eyes widened when she looked toward Bobsy's room. Her head tilted, and she tried to speak but couldn't. Mēkel turned to see what had her attention.

"Wow, my sister must be real important. What's your boyfriend doing here?" he asked, then turned and walked down the hall.

"Liam? What are you doing here?" Charly finally managed, speaking to herself, and zipping behind Mēkel.

Liam stood watching her. With each step she made closer to him, his eyes grew and a look of disbelief became a stare of horror. She hadn't made it all the way to the group before he bounded to meet her. Two feet in front of her, he stopped. His hands were in the air as if he were confused about being under arrest. "Charly love . . . what happened?" he asked, concerned and angry. His palms were still up. "Where were you?"

Charly smiled. "Do I look that bad?" She shook her head. "Never mind. Don't answer. I got us—me and Mēkel—stuck in the desert, probably totaled his hundred-thousand-dollar-plus rental car, which I have to pay for, then got us lost after I promised him I knew where I was going." She cheesed, big and wide. "And when it rains, it pours—literally, no cliché. That's why I'm drenched and dirty," she explained. "Why are you here? How'd you know where to come?"

Loud noise came from down the hall, stealing Charly and Liam's attention. She snaked her neck around him to get a good look, and was shocked by what she saw. Mēkel had lost his cool. He was yelling and pointing at Lex and Faizon, while Coop leaned against a wall behind them wearing a weird look. Eden stood between them, holding Mēkel back.

"And you want to know why I'm here?" Liam asked facetiously, indicating the altercation going on down the hall. "Well, that's why. That and you being on drugs is what made me hop the first flight I could get out of New York. Not to mention, I was supposed to be here in two days anyway. That's when the rest of the crew's coming."

"What?" She reared back her head. "Who's on drugs? What are you talking about, Liam? I've never done drugs in my life, unless you count sugar. That's the biggest drug on the planet."

"Get off me, Eden," she heard Mēkel's voice belt out. "I'm sorry, E. I didn't mean to raise my voice at you. You know how I feel about violence and females. I'm against it. I'm going to check on Bobsy," he said loud enough for everyone to hear.

Charly watched as Mēkel disappeared into a room she assumed belonged to Bobsy, then looked at Liam. "See what I'm talking about? I wasn't in danger—he's just the opposite of danger," she began, then changed her tune when Liam shot her a look. "Back to the drugs?"

Liam laughed. "Serious, love? You told me you were high when I called. That someone had given you something, put something illegal in your juice."

Now it was Charly's turn to laugh. Liam had misunderstood their conversation. He'd mistaken her having an energy rush from drinking too much of Lex's juice for her being slipped some kind of drugs, which definitely was not the case, and that was exactly what she was explaining when they were interrupted by Mēkel, who'd walked up minutes later.

"S'up?" He nodded to Liam, then looked into Charly's eyes. "Pardon me, Charly. Earlier, when I told you I chose and fought for you, I just want you to know I did that because you're excellent at what you do and from your other shows, I could tell your heart is in a good place. I listened—I mean, really listened—to you earlier when we were alone, and you giving away your purse to that girl, well, that confirmed it for me. I believe you were doing this for the right reasons. And you were kinda right." He put his hands on her shoulders and gazed intently as if they were the only two people in the world. "So what I'm doing now is not because of you—I want you to know that. My desires are much bigger than you said, but I avoid trouble." He put on an obviously false smile, stepped back, and began walking backward, still facing Charly. "You can keep the shirt. It looks better on you than it did on me." He turned and disappeared down the hall and exited through a door.

"What happened?" Charly almost yelled, walking away from Liam and down the hall toward the group.

"I'll tell you what happened," Lex growled, then shook his head. He looked at Faizon, then at Coop and locked eyes with him. He put his head down, then ran one hand over his hair, and turned around. He held up one finger. "I'm out! I need to run or something, knock out some of this frustration on a heavy bag, 'cause if I get in the ring, I'll hurt one of my trainers. Really bad. I don't wanna do that. Eden, Charly . . . I'll see you two at the camp." He turned toward Faizon. "Are you riding, Faizon? Coop?"

Faizon reached into his pocket and pulled out a key ring. "I got a rental, Golden Boy. And Coop's hopping on a bus headed to Cali, so I'm dropping him off on my way to the airport. We'll get up later, a'ight?" he said, then gave Lex a brotherly hug.

Lex nodded, then gave Coop a head nod. "Sorry, Coop. I tried. You know I did." He turned and walked opposite of the way that Mēkel had gone. "Let's go, Whip!" Whip scurried behind.

Faizon wore a frown that looked permanent. He grunted in frustration, then looked to Charly. He shrugged. "Pass me your phone so I can put my contact info in . . . just in case." Charly handed him her phone, and tried to piece together the broken puzzle of her day. She didn't know what was going on, but whatever it was, it was amiss. He handed her the cell, then pecked her on the cheek. "All right, mama. I guess I'll get up with you later. Another time, maybe another project." He turned away from her. "You ready, Coop?"

"What? What are you talking about? What happened?" Charly quizzed Faizon, then looked at Eden for explanation when he answered with silence.

Eden lost all her professional demeanor and just shrugged. "Mēkel isn't doing the project anymore, and Lex said he's quitting too. That's all I can say, Charly. There's a confidentiality clause in my contract. Sorry." She shrugged. "But I can talk to him—Lex, that is—and maybe change his mind." Eden teared up and dabbed her eyes. "But I can't leave you again. Look what happened to you when we rushed up here. Sorry, but I had to go . . . Bobsy."

"If you can change Lex's mind, Eden, you know where to find a bruh. I'm scheduled for the last flight out but, hopefully, I can hop an earlier one," Faizon said over his shoulder, then turned and walked and talked with Coop.

"Eden, you don't have to wait for Charly," Liam said, walking up and standing next to Charly. He put his arm around her shoulders. "I'll get her back to the camp."

Eden brightened, relief washing the worry from her face. "Really? Is that okay, Charly? I mean, I am supposed to be your chaperone."

"It's fine, just put your info and Lex's into my contacts too. That's the problem Mēkel and I had. We didn't know anyone's numbers, and wouldn't have known to come here if the crew at the Grime to Shine hadn't mentioned the hospital." She gave her phone to Eden and waited. "Go ahead, Eden. I need you to change Lex's mind more than I need you to wait for me. I'll catch up with you soon," she said, accepting her phone and giving Eden a quick one-armed hug. She turned to Liam. "I'll be back in a few. I'm going in here." She knocked lightly on Bobsy's door, then pushed it open and stuck in her head.

Charly needed to apologize to her, and she hoped she would accept.

Bobsy lay in the bed with her eyes closed. The lighting was dim, but warm and soft music filled the space. Charly took in the surroundings. There was nothing hospital-like about the room, but one thing was certain, Bobsy needed to be there. She was puny, and the twin bed she was tucked into dwarfed her.

"Hi, Charly," Bobsy said, opening her eyes. "Guess you know my secret now . . . why I couldn't come to the event? Why I wear a trainer's shirt, but don't train."

Charly shook her head, then adjusted a chair next to Bobsy's bed, so she could sit facing her. "No, actually I don't," she admitted, sitting. "What's your secret? If you don't mind telling me, that is."

Bobsy wiggled until she was sitting up. "Well, I'm not dying or anything. I have Marfan syndrome. You know a bit of scoliosis, mixed with a weak aorta—the main artery that carries blood from my heart . . . i.e. major heart problems, and major bone problems from being so thin. You know, yada yada yada?" Bobsy said, smiling like it wasn't a big deal, which Charly took as a cue from Bobsy not to make more of it than Bobsy wanted her to. "So basically I'm here again because my cardiologist was afraid I was going to suffer an 'aortic dissection,' " she said, holding up her fingers and making quote marks in the air. "That's when your aorta can burst—well, when someone else's can, but not mine. I'm too strong."

Charly reached over and held Bobsy's hand. "You certainly are . . ."

Bobsy shook her head. "Don't try to butter me up,

Charly. Remember, we're not friends," she reminded her with a smile in her voice. "Seriously, just spit it out. I don't like kiss-ups."

Charly nodded. "Cool. 'Cause I don't like kissing up." She paused. "I meant it when I said you're strong, and I hope you're strong enough to consider accepting my apology. It's just that you weren't wearing pink and had 'Trainer' on your shirt, and I'd never considered a female trainer—"

Bobsy laughed. "And my chest is major flat and my hair is cut like this. So you thought I was a boy. I get it. However, let's be clear." She angled her body more, facing Charly full on. "I didn't want my hair like this. I just kept getting hospitalized, wasn't thinking about combing it because I was concentrating on getting better, and, to top it off, I'd colored it and over-relaxed it—in the same day . . . major mistake." She shook her head. "It fell out. Now it's growing back. All that to say: yes, Charly, I accept your apology—we're still not friends though." She giggled again.

Charly laughed with her. "Okay, not-my-friend, I need something from you." Charly stood, then stepped next to Bobsy's bed. She waved her hand toward the mattress. "Mind if I sit here for a moment? I want to get a little personal." Bobsy nodded her permission, and Charly sat. She shared her life story with Bobsy, explained how her mother had been everything but a mother to her and her little sister, Stormy, while she was growing up, and then divulged her struggle. She'd worked for everything she had, including finding her father, who hadn't known where she was. Charly cried a little, admitting to Bobsy how more often than not, her mom had been out partying and gambling, while she and Stormy were missing daily essentials like electricity or food or money or a combination of two or more. She smiled when she spoke of her little sister's brilliance, then saddened, telling how there were many like her who would never be rewarded—saved—based on their being smart. Charly nodded. She'd told Bobsy everything.

"So . . . now you know my story—my secret. That's why I need your help. I want the guys to open up the center to more than just girls with medical illnesses; I want them to extend the project to include girls who fight other illnesses—inner dis-ease—like coming from the wrong side of the tracks, missing or inattentive parents . . ." She shrugged. "Poverties—mental, physical, and emotional, not just financial." Charly wiped her eyes, which had turned on like faucets. "I want to help girls like me . . . like who I was, and who I could've remained."

Bobsy stared at Charly, unblinking, like her brother, Mēkel. "You know what, Charly?" she asked, shaking her head in the negative. "I don't know how I can say this to you . . ." She scratched her head and looked away, mumbling under her breath, "You did call me bruh, like I was a boy." She looked Charly in the eyes. "Believe me, it really hurts more than anything to say this, but I have to, and I hope you understand."

She's getting ready to say no.

"First of all, you look awful. I can't believe you—not you, Charly St. James, the beautiful TV host, who dresses up American teens—are walking around looking like that. And you don't seem to be bothered by it at all." She shook her head again. "And if you add your background to the way you look now, not to mention you can't tell a girl from a boy, I'd have to say, your situation is worse than mine. And for that . . . I'm afraid, I was wrong. I didn't like you because I thought you were in this for you—for what you could get out of it, like a new spinoff show or more publicity. That's why I questioned you the day we met. That's why I needed to know what you said because I thought I'd been wrong about you. I've always liked your show, and admired you for helping others, but after I saw you and my brother fighting in the shoe store . . . well, I didn't trust you anymore." Bobsy shrugged. "So, okay, I'll say it twice: I was wrong. You're not stuck up and you don't think you're better than anyone, and I think we *can* be friends." She smiled. "I'll help you, Charly. You knew I would."

Charly exhaled. "Thank you, Bobsy. What about Mēkel? Why did he really walk away from the project? Him and Lex quit."

Bobsy shrugged. "Who knows? Probably because of Coop. It's always him and Coop battling. My mom used to say they were trying to see who could pee the furthest, meaning which one is the strongest. I always called it a battle between creativity and smarts. I don't need to tell you who's creative though. I bet it's because of Coop. I can work on finding out, but they're really good about keeping things from me. They don't want to stress me out." She rolled her eyes. "But don't worry about con-

vincing Mēkel. I can do that. You just worry about finding him. I warn you though, he's good at hiding when
he's upset—especially now that my cardiologist has
cleared me, he'll feel like he can disappear for a while.
When you do find him, Charly, ask him if he's ever been
stuck between a dollar and a dream. I won't say more
than that, but that'll trigger him."

14

Liam wasn't trying to hear one word of Charly's plan, and was blatantly clear about it. He followed closely behind her, stepping on her heels and expressing his disproval as they walked down the hospital corridor. Charly looked over her shoulder, rolling her eyes like a child. She had no other way of relating her contempt for him or his thinking he really had some say with how she conducted her life, unless she resorted to throwing expletives at him. But she was practicing controlling herself, and didn't want to curse him out, though she'd been tempted each time he said, "No, I won't have it!" Stopping in front of the elevator bank, she pressed the call button and waited for its arrival. Crossing her arms, she tapped her foot and felt the water from her soaked sneakers squish around her toes. *Why can't he just shut up?* she thought, as a ding announced the elevator's arrival, and the doors parted, allowing their entrance.

"Good evening," she greeted the few riders, who were looking at her like she was an escapee from the thirteenth floor—the psychiatric floor in every hospital she knew about. She gave herself a once-over, and understood why they were gawking the way they were. If mental stability could be judged by looks, she had to admit she didn't appear behaviorally healthy, especially with Liam standing next to her, accusing her of being insane. Ignoring him, she opened her Contacts on her phone and found Faizon's info.

ME: This is Charly. I'm going to Cali tonight too.

Faizon replied almost immediately.

FAIZON: That's whuzzup, mama! You can crash at my crib! ☺ You booked a flight?

ME: Doing it now! ☺

Charly texted back, then sent a message to Eden asking if she could go with her to California and if Eden would book their flights and pack her a purse.

Liam leaned in, trying to read over her shoulder. "You know you're crazy, Charly?"

"I am insane, Liam," she finally broke her silence, staring him down. He'd pushed her past patience, and she couldn't maintain control anymore. "In sane—two words, get it? I'm in my sanity, which is why I have to go. How else will this project succeed?" she asked, watching the numbers above the doors light up as they descended to the lobby.

The elevator doors opened. "Who told you it's your job to make sure this happens, love?" Liam asked as he stood to the side, gesturing for her to step off before him. "Never mind. I already know the answer to that. But I'm going with," he said, inviting himself on her journey as he traveled behind her down the hallway. "There's no way I'm allowing you to chase behind some dude. Alone. One who doesn't too much care for you, I might add." He slow jogged in front of her, holding open the exit door for her as she walked out of the hospital.

Charly turned on her heels. "I'm going to act like I didn't just hear you say that. Allow? Really!" Her voice rose with each word, drawing the attention of passersby and hospital staff. "You're right; I put myself in charge of making this project happen, and if it doesn't happen, we don't get a new spinoff show. But I also need this, Liam. Me—well, other girls like me need it. If I'd had a place to go and I'd had support like the retreat is going to offer, do you know how much I would have benefited when I was pretty much on my own before I was reunited with my father? Do you realize what that would've done for a girl whose mother was not there?" she asked, then walked over to the hired car Liam had waiting just off the entrance. "As harsh as it sounds, Mēkel, Lex, and Faizon opening a place just for fighters and survivors of diseases isn't enough. Other girls need a safe haven too, and I'm going to make sure they get it," she stated, getting into the car and settling into her seat, while Liam got in next to her and shut the door. "So you can object all you want, accuse me of chasing behind Mēkel. . . . I don't care. *I* am going, you're not."

"Why not? What's so wrong with me going with you?" Liam asked, his voice heavy with frustration.

Charly looked at him. "Because you need this just as much as I do, but for a different reason. For me, it's personal, and for you, it's business. And business is business is business, and you know like I know that this can help skyrocket our careers. The stats of viewers—the Nielsen ratings—will be phenomenal, just like the product endorsements that we know will come in." She shook her head, then put her hand on his arm, hoping to woo him. "So you can't go. You need to stay here and work on Lex, get him back in the game. He's athletic, you're athletic. He's driven, you're driven. Use your similarities to appeal to him," she pleaded in a soft voice, a sweet tone she knew he'd have a hard time rejecting.

Liam's face told her that he was considering her words. "I don't know. I'm not comfortable with you traveling to Cali alone."

Charly gave him a soft sincere smile. "But I'm not going alone, Liam. That's what Eden's for," she said and thought, *if she can go with me.* She turned her head and looked out the window as the car drove away. Her phone vibrated, momentarily stealing her attention and making her smile.

EDEN: All packed! DELTA, last flight. I'll meet you at the airport.

Faizon's house was ridiculously palatial, Charly thought as she sat next to his infinity pool, staring out at the Pacific, which twinkled under the blanket of stars. The day had been hectic, but being surrounded by so much water relaxed her, which was exactly what she was aiming for. Her body was exhausted, but mentally and emotionally, she was tired, and should've already gone to bed like Eden. It seemed as if the last week had been negatively affected by the opposite sex, giving her a brand-new definition of boy crazy. She straightened the folder on her lap, which kept blowing open with the salty scented breeze.

"You good, mama?" Faizon asked, startling her.

With a hand to her heart, she exhaled. "You can't sneak up on me, Faizon. You might mess around and catch a beat down at your own house," she joked.

He laughed with her, and held out his hand to her. "C'mon, mama. Let's go take a walk."

Charly protested, pointing to the folder. "I can't."

Faizon reached down, grabbing her hand. He pulled her up effortlessly. "Trust, you can do whatever you want. Can is an—"

"Ability," she finished for him, setting the folder down in the lounge chair she'd be sitting on. "But I have to work. I have to finish this project."

He nodded. "Right to your first statement; can is an ability, mama. Wrong to your second; the project is a wrizzap, Charly. A wrap," he said again, as if she didn't understand what wrizzap meant. "Mēkel walked, Lex is done because Mēkel walked. What more can you do tonight?" He waved his hand toward the expanse surrounding them. "How can you ignore all of this? You're not here to work—not tonight. You can't hunt Mēkel down until the morning. Besides, you'll have plenty to do then, when we . . . ," he began, then stopped and looked out into the distance where the sound of the tide rushing in interrupted him. "I never get tired of hearing that. It's one of the reasons I'll never give up living on the coast."

"When we what? You were saying something," Charly reminded him.

He looked back at her. "When we see Mēkel. You don't have to hunt him down. I know where he is. Rather, where he'll be. I start filming tomorrow, and he's meeting me on the set so we can chop it up. Ya know, talk. "

Her eyes widened. "Really?"

Faizon nodded. "Yeah, and you'll be there too. You do want to see ya boy in his glory, right? See how movies are made? So now you can relax, mama. Enjoy yourself, especially since it's only me, you, and Eden. My grandmother's out of town."

Charly yawned, then nodded because she didn't know what else to do. She was super excited that she wouldn't have to hunt down Mēkel, but didn't know if it would be appropriate for her to be alone in the house with Faizon. She wondered if she should go to a hotel, but then thought better of it. She needed Faizon. He was the only one out of the three who hadn't walked away from the project, which told her she had a chance of getting him to help her with Mēkel, especially since Mēkel was visiting him on the movie set. She also knew that Faizon knew the real reasons for the blow-up between Mēkel and Lex, and those were critical for her to know if she planned on fixing the problem. "Okay, okay, and okay," she said, acquiescing with hidden intention, and telling herself she'd be fine. Eden was with her, so they weren't really alone, and she wasn't attracted to Faizon personally. She was just infatuated with what he did. She was intrigued by his artistry, she told herself, as she gripped his hand and let him lead her to the beach. She yawned again, this time removing her hand from his, and stretching her fingertips to the sky.

"You're really tired," he said after she'd finished stretching. He took her hand in his again, lacing his fingers through hers. "C'mon, mama. Let's get you inside. You can sleep in my bed." He pulled her toward the house.

Charly's eyes stretched. "No, no, that's okay," she protested. "And it wouldn't be right."

Faizon laughed softly, leading her up a small hill that stretched to his house. "Nah, it wouldn't be right. It would fantastic," he flirted. "But that's not what I'm suggesting, mama. You can have my bedroom—you and Eden. She's already in there asleep. It's big and has its own bathroom. I'll crash in the guest room." He led her across the walk and onto his deck.

Charly followed him, then stopped next to the infinity pool, where he picked up her folder. "Are you sure? I don't want to put you out."

Faizon leaned in, then planted a soft kiss on her cheek. "Charly, I guess you have selective vision. You see only what you want to see. You're not putting me out, you're reeling me in." He kissed her face again, then backed up. "My room is up the stairs, the last door on the right. I have to go . . . before I say or do something stupid. I can't be who I am if I'm blowing my cool over a girl." He winked and turned away. "I'll see you in the morning, mama."

Charly stood there, questioning what she'd just heard. She'd reeled in Faizon and hadn't even tried. She only hoped it would work to her advantage.

15

The room was moving. An earthquake, she was sure. Her eyes popped open in panic, causing her immediate regret. Blinding bright sunlight filtered through the floor-to-ceiling windows, assaulting her pupils and making her wince. She blinked slowly, trying to adjust her vision. She had to see what was happening, had to figure out what to do. The floor was vibrating and the bed shook. She grabbed the sides of her head, which was hurting, and discovered that her temples throbbed too. She looked left, then right, searching for Eden, but she was nowhere to be found. All she saw was a huge painting on the wall, shaking from the movement. A loud crash, one louder than she'd ever heard, made her scramble to her feet.

"Eden!" she yelled, looking down at the floor that should've been still, but wasn't. "Eden! Faizon!" she screamed again when the floor started making noises too. *I have to be having a nightmare*, she thought when she heard the hardwood hum, then felt it vibrate. It felt like she was standing on top of a huge concert speaker, feeling the bass blow.

"Charly! Charly! What is it? You okay?" Eden said, bursting through the door with a frying pan in her hand, an oven mitt on her hand and a full apron over what appeared to be a tank top. A lot of noise followed her into the bedroom.

Charly tilted her head. "An earthquake—" she began, then jumped. Another loud crash sounded and her eyes widened in panic. "Oh my god, the windows are breaking. How big is the quake?"

Eden laughed, shaking her head. Faizon popped his head into the room, looking around. "What's so funny?" he asked. "Charly, did I hear you call my name? Were you just screaming, mama?"

Eden was almost doubled over in laughter. "Charly thinks we're having an earthquake."

Faizon walked all the way into the room, looking like he'd been dipped in money. His clothes were top-of-the-line flashy. The wild long hair he'd had just hours before had been expertly fashioned into dreadlocks. "Pre-film party," he announced, smiling. "I always have one before I begin taping. It gets my adrenaline flowing."

Eden held the frying pan. "The caterers are downstairs, set up on the deck next to the pool, but Faizon prefers my pancakes. I make great waffles too though. Which do you prefer, pancakes or waffles?"

Charly looked around. *Caterers?* She held up her arm, glanced at her wrist for her watch, then remembered it wasn't there. "What time is it?"

"It's still early. It's barely nine. I don't have to be at the set until eleven because I have my own groomers, and the studio sends over my wardrobe. I'll see you downstairs," Faizon said, backing out of the room.

Another loud crash sounded, making Charly jump. "What's that noise?"

Faizon smiled. "You don't wanna know, mama. C'mon, Eden, let's let Charly get dressed. See you downstairs on the deck."

There were naked girls in the pool. Nude. Completely minus clothes and self-respect, Charly thought as she stuck her cell phone in her pocket and walked through the house, looking at the groupies through the floor-to-ceiling windows. The house had transformed from Faizon's home into a makeshift daytime club. Music blasted, food and drinks were being served, and at least a hundred people were everywhere she looked. Some were dancing, others were mingling, and in the far corner of the room, a group of guys was betting on a video game match. She scratched her head, trying to make sense of it all. How could Faizon prepare to film with so much ruckus around him?

The sound of breaking glass vibrated throughout the room, making her jump and pulling her attention. It was the same sound that had scared her when she'd awoken from her slumber. Charly watched the group of video gamers and gamblers. Two were holding controls, while the others were huddled in front of the huge flat screen, kneeling and throwing money down on the floor. The crash whooshed through the hidden surround-sound speakers again, and they jumped in the air, pumping their fists and screaming as a virtual screen shattered, apparently announcing a winner.

"Are you kidding me?" she said with a hand on her hip. "Seriously? Video game heads and naked girls right before going to the set? Irresponsible."

"You're telling me. They've been at it all morning too," Eden said, walking up to her with a plate stacked with pancakes. She turned her face away from the food and yawned. "Sorry. Here, take this and eat something before we leave. Faizon will be ready soon. He's talking to Mēkel."

Charly perked up. "Mēkel? Where are they?"

Eden shook her head. "He's not here. Faizon's in the back room on the phone. Well, at least he was, but I guess not anymore," she said, motioning toward the patio doors, where Faizon was entering.

"There you are, sleepy head. Welcome to Party Central!" Faizon greeted her as if he hadn't just seen her minutes before. "You ready to go? You should grab your things and put on some shoes. We have to leave like right now." He looked at his watch, then shook his head. He turned to the crowd. " 'Ey yo! It's time!" he yelled. "I gotta get to the set!"

Charly watched everyone ignore him and held her breath. She was sure that at any moment he was going to snap. The video gamers told him their game wasn't done yet, and they weren't leaving until it was, and the people who were dancing continued to dance. "I can help you," she offered, heading toward the deck. She didn't have time to wait for Faizon's party crew. She had to get to the set so she could see Mēkel. "Okay, ladies. It's time to get moving. We have work to do."

One of the nude girls lying next to the pool on a patio chaise longue, turned to Charly. She lifted the one item she wore—her sunglasses, and looked at Charly through bright blue contacts. "We're not leaving until the caterers finish our omelets. Why don't you take off your clothes and jump in the pool with the others. You're no more special than the rest of us. Especially me. I have seniority. That means I've been here the longest, so Faizon lets me do whatever I want." She eased her sunglasses back down, then turned her head as if Charly hadn't spoken.

Before Charly knew it, her feet had carried her to the side of the pool. "I know what seniority means!" Her hands were on the side of the chaise longue, and her body weight was against it. With one hard football player's charge, she'd rolled Blue Contacts into the pool with the patio lounge following her. "You may've been here the longest, but I have the upper hand. I said get out!" Charly yelled, grabbing a nearby bottle of beer that she couldn't believe they were drinking. "Or I'm going to start busting heads." A few girls got up without protest, and a couple others sat there with their chins dropped toward their chests in disbelief.

"That's Charly! Did you see the video of her attacking Mēkel? She's crazy," Charly overhead one of the girls unsuccessfully attempt to whisper to another. Her cell phone vibrated in her pocket.

"Oh yeah. I'm crazy. And I'm going to show you crazy too, as soon as I get back." After she threw the empty threat, she went back inside to answer her phone, hoping they'd think she was coming back with something more threatening than a beer bottle. She bounded the stairs two by two, headed to Faizon's bedroom. She'd just closed the door behind her, when the vibration stopped, indicating she'd missed a call. She slipped into her shoes and grabbed her purse, then reached inside her pocket and retrieved the phone. She shook her head. She'd missed Liam's call, but didn't feel like talking to him or answering his handful of questions that were laced with insecurity or jealousy or, worse, his thinking she had to answer to him. She huffed. As much as she wanted to ignore him, she couldn't. He was supposed to be appealing to Lex to make the project happen, and she was supposed to be finding Mēkel. They both had a new show on the line that was dependent on the guys' retreat for girls being a major success, so, there was no getting around communicating with Liam. They were in this together.

"Yes, Liam?" she greeted him when he answered.

"He's gone. Lex is gone!" Liam was out of breath.

Charly tilted her head. "What do you mean 'he's gone'? Try the hills—that's where he runs. If he's not there, he has to be in the gym. He can't leave the training camp. His Showtime event is, like, tomorrow or the next day or something," she said, exaggerating. Lex wasn't scheduled to fight so soon, but it seemed like it was right around the corner.

"No, Charly. He's gone. Like out-there-in-Cali gone. It seems he went back to his old stomping ground—a different training camp—because he couldn't focus here."

Charly nodded.

Faizon burst into the room. "I can't get them to leave, and we gotta go," he muttered.

Charly put a hand on her hip and rolled her eyes. She covered the cell mic, then whispered to Faizon, "Where's your fuse box?" He shrugged. She waved her hand at him. "Just go. I'll get with you in a minute," she said, disgusted, then turned her attention back to Liam. "Text me the address here, and I'll go get him."

"No, no, you won't. Whip said it's crazy dangerous, even in the daytime. He said the cops won't even go without backup because the neighborhood's so rough," Liam protested.

Charly blew her frustration. "Listen, Liam, do you want this spinoff show or not? Because I do, and I'm going to do whatever it takes to get it. You just go build something or wait for the rest of the crew to get there." She hung up on him, then marched out of the bedroom. She jogged down the stairs, turned a couple of corners in the house, and finally found the garage. "Voila!" she stated, finding the fuse box. With one pull of the door and one click of the main power switch, she did what Faizon couldn't: she made the partiers leave, because it was hard to party, play games, or cook without electricity.

16

Faizon was no longer just Faizon—he was beautiful, she told herself. She sat in his cast chair next to Eden, watching him intently on one of the camera's screens. For a brief moment, she'd gotten so wrapped up in him that she had forgotten she'd come to the set to see Mēkel, whenever he showed. Despite Faizon's early-morning partying and inability to control his friends, she respected his artistry. He switched lives in front of the cameras, becoming the character that he portrayed. Charly thought it was a great role for him because it was hard to distinguish fiction from reality. "This is great," she whispered to Eden. "He can get an Oscar for this if he stays in character. It's like I don't even see Faizon on the set. All I see is whoever he's playing."

Eden sat next to Charly, shaking her head, while Charly toyed with the all-access studio pass around her neck she'd been issued, and checked the time. "It's not his best, not the part. He should've won for his last film—it was more positive. Kind of like Denzel Washington back in the day. Remember he won an Oscar for being a dirty cop, but not Malcolm X or one of his other positive roles? The media never recognizes our community when we play positive parts. They only highlight thug roles."

Charly cringed. Eden was a little accurate and a lot wrong, and her uneducated views irritated Charly. Yes, the media hadn't given their community a fair shake or the credit it deserved. All one had to do to know that was look at ratios of people on television or writers on bookstore shelves and bestseller lists or actors in movies. The lack of recognition Charly could agree with, but not the roles. She looked at her watch for the umpteenth time in ten minutes, then turned to Eden. "The Oscar isn't won based upon what *kind* of film it is, Eden. It's based upon suspension of disbelief—how well the actor plays the part. Remember when Jamie Foxx played Ray Charles, and we forgot that we were watching Jamie because we didn't see him anymore, and we only saw Ray?" Eden nodded. "Well that's why he won the Oscar. No different from the movie *Precious*."

Eden nodded. "Okay, I get it now. I'll have to remember that the next time I see a script." She looked at her watch. "It's almost time for them to break, Charly." She lifted her brows, giving Charly a look of concern.

Charly nodded, wondering why Eden would be reading scripts, then shrugged. "I know. I know. I'm on it. Mēkel has to show up soon," she wished aloud. "Another thing, where is Lex's camp here? Do you have an address or can you take me there?"

Eden looked down, then shook her head. "I can't, Charly. I got a text from Lex earlier, and Faizon told me to mind my business." She pressed her lips together. "I wish I could, but . . . you know. Work."

"You work for him and signed a confidentiality clause, yada yada yada. I heard it before," Charly hissed, borrowing Bobsy's yadas. "It's old. And worse, it's going to get in the way of the project. But it's cool though, if you don't want to help girls like Bobsy . . ." She left the rest hanging in the air, hoping Eden would feel some sort of guilt and spill Lex's whereabouts.

Eden just sat there looking straight ahead. "But Faizon . . ."

The bell sounded, signaling the break had come. Faizon made his way over to them with a pronounced limp and a million-dollar smile. "Well, what did you guys think? Charly? Eden? How am I doing?" he asked, his words now proper and his enunciation perfect.

Charly's brows drew together in wonder, then rose in surprise. Faizon didn't sound like himself. She'd never heard him speak so eloquently or not end his sentences with *mama*. "What happened to your leg?" she asked. "Did you hurt it after we got here, because you weren't limping earlier. And why can't Eden tell me where Lex is?"

Faizon's million-dollar smile turned trillion-dollar brilliant. "Ahh, you noticed. Huh, mama? I'm uppin' my swag. Turnin' up for the miz-oovie," he said with a bit too much passion, making what Charly assumed he considered street lingo sound like certified Ebonics, a term she thought was stupid. He'd also ignored her question about Lex.

She rolled her eyes. "You're trying too hard with the vernacular, Faizon. No one will ever take you seriously speaking like that. Who talks that way, anyway?" she was saying when a different bell sounded. "So about Lex's camp?"

Faizon stuck his hand in his pocket, and pulled out a set of keys. He tossed them to Charly. "Sorry, I have to run. Please hold those for me. I forgot to put them away with the rest of my things." He waved at them both. "That bell's my cue. I have to go back now and rehearse some lines." He nodded. "We just broke for a quick restroom break." He pointed behind him with his thumb. "It seems not everyone around here can keep their bladders in check. Too many potty breaks!" he said, switching dialects again as he shuffled back to the set and disappeared behind a black curtain.

Charly's jaw dropped. Either L.A. was really La-La land or she'd been hearing things. Had Faizon really just said "potty"? She looked at Eden, who didn't seem the least bit fazed, and questioned her authenticity too. "You know, Eden, about you working for Lex . . . did he hire you or did the network hire you?" Charly asked, fitting more pieces of the puzzle together and putting Faizon's keys into her purse.

Eden put on her model-like smile again. "Well, it's because of Lex that I'm your chaperone, if that's what you're asking. But, really it's because of Faizon. He came up with the fabulous idea, then told Lex about it."

"What?" Charly asked, now really confused. "Idea?"

Faizon's head popped around the black curtain.

"Eden, I think you're going to be a shoo-in. I just told the producer about your part in the play. He's thinking of speaking to you. Now I have to go run lines. I had the times mixed up. I should've been here earlier." He disappeared again.

Charly stared at her. "You're an actress? I thought you were Lex's cousin."

Eden shrugged. "I'm an actress and a chaperone and Lex's fake cousin. I'm from his old neighborhood, and we've known each other since preschool, so his family looks out for me. Plus, I have to make money while I'm working on my craft. So, today, I'm a chaperone."

Charly shook her head. "That means today you're essentially working for me, not Lex and not Faizon. The network's paying you; they hired you off of Lex's recommendation." Eden nodded slightly. "So, I guess you can go back to Las Vegas or wherever then, Eden. You abandoned me, and I got lost and stuck in the desert. Then you wouldn't tell me why the show was at risk when Lex and Mēkel got into it, and now you won't tell me where the camp is. As my chaperone, you're supposed to make sure I get to where I need to safely and on time." Charly pasted on a false smile. "And while all those instances may not have fit within your title, I'm sure the network will take my side. Business is business, and you, Eden, you're fired for insubordination. Take care," Charly said without apology or remorse or anger. She got up, and speed walked through one of the doors. She didn't know her way, but would find it. The only thing that concerned her at the moment was making a call.

"Are you with someone?" a young blond guy who looked no older than Charly asked, while looking at the all-access visitor's pass Charly's wore.

Charly nodded. "Yes, I'm here with Faizon, but I'm looking for an ex—"

"Right back there." He pointed, cutting her off and walking away. "Second door on your left. Enter quietly because he's rehearsing lines."

Ready to get answers about Mēkel's whereabouts or where she could find him, Charly walked toward the second door. Eden refused to talk, but that wouldn't be the case with Faizon. If he couldn't handle the situation at his home, he surely wasn't ready to take her on, she decided, rushing through the rehearsal door with all her might. She dug her feet in the floor, and stuck out her hands to prevent herself from colliding with the brick wall she'd almost walked face-first into. "Oh." She smiled, admiring the structure that wasn't a wall at all, but a life-like studio prop that was set on wheels.

" 'Nah'mean?" Faizon said from somewhere behind the fake brick wall, pulling Charly's attention. "I ain't no window dressing, son. I was born in Kingston, raised in Queens, and I know how to get down for mine. I'm mean with these thangs. Nah'mean?" Faizon rattled one sentence after another, inflecting harder and harder.

"Good. Good. Faizon. You've perfected the nah'mean. Very authentic! Now let's try the line from the love scene. How about we go over that?" someone who Charly thought was a voice coach said.

"Sure. We can go over the love scene. I practiced that one so many times, I couldn't help but master it," Faizon said in a voice that Charly knew had to be his true one. "Yo, mama, you got selective vision, you know that? Meaning, you only see what you wanna see. So see this: You're good for me, ma. With other women . . . it was like they were pushin' a playa outta the game; but with you . . . you're pushin' the game outta the playa. So see, you're not pushing me out, you're reelin' me in."

"What the *what!*" Charly said, way louder than she'd planned. "Really? Almost word for word too."

"Charly, is that you?" Faizon's voice called out. "One second," he said to the coach.

She heard the scraping of a chair being dragged across the floor, followed by footsteps and other clanking noises. The brick wall rolled to the side, and Faizon appeared, wearing a proud grin. "So, you like it, mama? Don't ya?" he said, snapping his fingers like he'd just thought of something.

Her eyes were surely going to pop out of her skull, Charly thought. She could feel them protrude just like she felt her nostrils expand and her fists ball. She borrowed Mēkel's philosophy. *Control. Control the situation more than you let the situation control you.* "You're serious, huh?" she asked Faizon. "So this whole time I've known you, every conversation we've had . . . it was all a joke? Just like Eden being a chaperone? That's your idea of acting?"

Faizon laughed and waved her question away. "No, Charly, it wasn't a joke. I was perfecting my character. I always do that. I live as the character until I finish filming. It's the only way to come across authentic. You have to really become the part," Faizon explained. "I can help you when you decide to cross over from the small screen to the big one—"

Her palms were on his chest. His body flew backward, crashing against the brick wall prop. And Charly's finger was pointed in his face and her breath spurted out before she knew it. "Help me? You could've helped me by telling me the truth, Faizon! And just think, I believed you. So no Kingston to Queens to Las Vegas to Hollywood. No fighting to survive. No really liking me." She threw her arms up in frustration. "And probably no Mēkel either. Everything's been a lie, including your mother dying from—"

"My mother did die from cancer, Charly," he interrupted. His tone was bleak, and his eyes weren't bright with pride anymore. "I didn't lie to you . . . not about everything. Okay, so I fluffed the truth a bit about Mēkel. But that was only because I wanted you with me. I wanted you to see me work. But my mother . . . I wish that was a lie. I lost her a couple of months ago." He reached out to touch Charly, and she pulled away. "I do like you—that's why I wanted you here. I'm really into you."

Charly shook her head. "No, Faizon. You're really into you—into yourself. I get the perfecting-the-character part, but you shouldn't play on people's emotions or play games with other people's lives. Those girls back in Las Vegas need this project, and you couldn't care less," she said, then turned on her heel and left the way she'd come in. She moved quickly down the hall, searching for a red exit sign above the few doors she spotted. She had to get away. Quick. Hollywood had gifts for her she didn't want, like Faizon, the pretend boy from the hood, and Eden, the sham of an actress who couldn't act like a chaperone.

"I gotta get out of here," she said. "I don't care how dangerous a place Lex is in, I'd rather deal with reality any day." She ran down the hall, and finally found her way out of the huge building.

Jogging slowly through the lot of studios, searching for the place where they'd parked, she dug into her purse for Faizon's keys. He'd tricked her into coming to the studio, so she decided that having him provide her a way out—his car—was only fair. She had to get to Lex, and she still had to find Mēkel. She shook her head, following the arrow on a sign that pointed toward the lot. Her cell phone vibrated against the back of her hand, and she breathed a mini sigh of relief. She didn't know who was calling, but suddenly she didn't feel so alone. She whipped out the cell, and saw her best friend's name scroll across the screen.

"Lola," she answered, breathlessly, tilting her head to secure the cell between her shoulder and ear while she continued to run. "I'm in Hollywood, I think. And I'm lost. Terribly lost. I don't know where Mēkel is, and Lex has gone MIA on Liam. I need him too. Everything is crazy."

"Hold up! Hold up! What are you talking about, Charly?" Lola said, popping gum in Charly's ear. "And this better be better than the news I'm calling to tell you."

Charly turned right and almost ran into a dressing rack of clothes. She felt like she was in some cheesy Hollywood movie, in which some comedy actor couldn't find his way through the maze, and ended up running through set designs that resembled cities or sky or something. "Excuse me," she said, her head still tilted. "Okay, Lola, here it is." She filled her friend in on the happenings, and finally found the lot. She pressed the remote to unlock the doors, and instead, the car roared to life. She selected another button on the key, and another, then started pushing down two at a time until she heard the locks click open. "So I have to find them. I just don't know who to get to first." She tossed her purse onto the passenger's seat, got into the car, took off the all-access pass and stuck it into her purse, then put on the seat belt.

Lola laughed as if Charly had just cracked the best joke of her lifetime. "That's easy, Charly. Don't tell me you've become such a big celebrity that you've forgotten how to do things for yourself," Lola said, and Charly could hear her typing in the background. "We're like Generation Y or Z or something, so that means the Internet is our best friend. Here!" she shouted. "Mēkel has a concert tonight, and Lex is . . . uh . . . let's see. Aha!" she exclaimed, and Charly's hopes rose. "Ah, it's nothing. He's scheduled for a Showtime interview, but not for days. And you know the interviews always come *after* the fights, so you have plenty of time."

Charly stuck the key into the ignition and pressed the start button. "Got it, Lola. Thanks," she said, then put the car in gear and tapped the accelerator. The car shot forward, and Charly slammed the brake pedal to the floor. Her purse toppled off of the seat, and its contents spilled. Beads of sweat popped across her forehead and her heart thumped. She was probably less than an inch from crashing into the truck in front of her. Carefully, she put the car in P, and reached over to pick up her things and toss them back into her purse. Her eyes lit up when she saw her open wallet. Coop's business card. Coop had told her if she ever needed anything, he'd be there for her. She knew he'd taken a bus into Cali the same night she'd flown in, so, hopefully, he was still there. She knew she didn't have to question whether Coop was the real thing or not; his facial tattoos and Mēkel's description of Coop's past told her he was authentic. She only hoped he lived up to his word. "Lola, I think I'm good. Now I just have to find my way back to Faizon's, and that should be easy. Either his address is in his navigation system or it's online." Charly breathed easily now. "I'll call you when I get to Faizon's. I don't want to be on the phone while I'm driving."

Lola cleared her throat. "Charly, you know I don't work for you, right? I didn't call to assist you. I called to tell you that we're going to be neighbors. I'm moving to New York!" Lola announced, then sneezed. "Isn't that great? Maybe I can work on your new show."

Charly agreed. It was terrific news. It would also be terrific if she got the new show, but right now it didn't look like that was going to happen. But she wasn't giving up so easy. "Time to call in the troops," she muttered, then hung up with Lola and dialed Coop.

17

Charly sat by the infinity pool, looking out at the ocean and waiting for Coop. Her purse was on the patio table, her phone was in her lap, and her hopes were everywhere except high. She'd been waiting on him almost two hours, and was growing restless. She needed to get to Lex and Mēkel, but more than that, she needed to get inside of Faizon's house to retrieve her things. She had no idea where she was going or how she was going to get back to Las Vegas or when, but she knew she couldn't stay at Faizon's a minute more. He and Eden were too wishy-washy for her. Neither seemed to know who he or she was, but lived in character moments. He was whomever he was playing, and Eden was whomever someone else wanted her to be to earn a paycheck.

A slamming noise came from the side of the house that sounded like a gate closing, and Charly's shoulders relaxed. She'd told Coop where to find her, and like he'd promised, he'd shown.

"Charly," Coop greeted from behind. "I got here as fast as I could. I didn't know if you were still here or not because I didn't see Faizon's car outside. What's up? You ready?" he asked, walking toward her.

She turned in her seat and smiled. He still looked like death getting ready to happen—from his tattoos and permanent grimace—but it was an appearance she now welcomed. She laughed inside, thinking how life took its own turns and made you follow. The guy she'd been wary of had turned into someone she'd looked forward to seeing. She stood up. "Thanks, Coop! Thanks for being a man of your word. No, even more than that, thanks for being you. I used the garage opener and parked Faizon's car inside. I left the keys in the ignition too. I just borrowed it to get here. I didn't want him to think I stole it. I don't want any more run-ins with police."

She shook her head. "Long story. Me and Whip were stopped the other day."

Coop stopped in his tracks. His look went from dangerous to confused. "Makes sense. So why are you thanking me for being me? Who else did you expect me to be?"

Charly threw her hands up in surrender. "It's just that nobody is who I thought they were," she said, then went on to vent about Faizon being the actor of the year, Eden being the wannabe actress/chaperone, Lex being the number-one contender who'd turned into a quitter, and

Mēkel having a male hissy fit because control had turned into uncontrollable.

Coop lit up, then doubled over in laughter, shocking Charly. She hadn't known he had a light side to him. "You don't know who you're talking about, Charly. You talk about them all as if they're separate people, when you should be viewing them as the same."

Her head tilted in wonder. "Huh? I don't get it."

Coop waved his hand, beckoning for her to follow him. "Didn't you tell me on the phone that you can't get your stuff because of Fai's alarm system?" he asked, cutting Faizon's name in half. "Well, come on. I can help you. There's not an alarm I can't crack." Charly hesitated, and her concern must've registered on her face. "Don't worry, I got you. And if the cops do show up— which they won't, because I know what I'm doing—I won't go to jail anyway. Faizon will just tell them I'm supposed to be here because he knows better."

Charly didn't like the sound of his implied threat. "Maybe we shouldn't. I can just get my things later."

Coop shrugged, then continued to walk. "Your call, but if I was you . . . I'd snatch up my stuff. You never know who'll be in it. Faizon likes to party, if you don't know yet."

Charly followed him to the side of the house, and her eyes stretched. On the ground lay a small metal box that had wires stretching up from it that were connected to other wires in a panel on the side of Faizon's house. A digital pad was next to it. "What's this?" she asked, wondering if this was the genius part of Coop that Mēkel had referred to.

Coop laughed again. "I told you I was cracking the alarm code. See?" he said, then pressed a few buttons until the digital display read DISARMED. He looked at her, then pushed the digits again, reactivating Faizon's security system. "You sure you don't want your stuff?"

Charly shook her head. "Yes," she said, her words opposite of her actions. She wanted her things, but not badly enough to do a break and enter. "I do want it. Can you go in and get it? I don't want to break in. It's in Faizon's room." Coop's brows rose, and Charly gave him a side eye. "Don't play me, Coop. I didn't stay in Faizon's room with Faizon. That's not my style. Me and Eden slept in there. My luggage is black with wheels, and I have some toiletries on his sink." She crossed her arms, then walked off. "Thanks again. I'll be in your car waiting for you."

The old beat-up Chevy hummed down the Pacific Coast Highway, headed in a direction Charly didn't know. The music on the system was old and streamed through much older speakers that popped every so often. "All right, so we need to get you to Lex," Coop said, cruising as if he didn't have a care in the world. "First though, I need to make a stop. We gotta gear up." He exited off the highway.

Charly manually rolled up her window. "Gear up how?" she asked with a hint of fear. Coop was a felon, and she wasn't certain that he was as legal as he proclaimed he now was.

Coop turned a corner, then pointed. "There. That's where we're going for ammunition."

"Oh. No. No, I'm not!" Charly protested. "I said I was from both sides of the street, Coop. I didn't say I play in the street. I can't be doing illegal stuff!"

The Chevy's tires screamed as Coop maneuvered the car to the curb and jerked to a halting stop. His stare was deathly cold. "I thought you said you wanted this. You needed this. Ain't that what you told me on the phone? 'Help me, Coop. I need you, Coop,'" he sang in heart-wrenching tone. "Now you acting all scared." He paused, glaring. "So now you got my attention, tell me, do you want this or not? And why? What's in it for you, Charly? Everybody wants something, and nobody works for free. So what's in it?"

Charly gulped. She was sitting in a car with a convicted criminal who probably knew the streets better than she knew how to breathe, so she knew she couldn't lie to him. He'd see through it. "Opportunity," she admitted. "At first it was the opportunity, the opportunity to help, and then it was a bigger opportunity—a new show. If I could pull it off, I could design their other retreats across the country."

Coop nodded, drumming on the steering wheel just like Mēkel had when they had been trying to find their way to Bobsy. "Okay. Money. I can respect that."

"No. No," Charly stopped him. "I said 'at first.'"

"That's bull, Charly. It's always the money. You know it. I know it. Everybody knows it!"

Charly drew her brows together. "How are you going to tell me about me, Coop?" she asked, more agitated than afraid. She remembered Mēkel saying Coop was a genius and Bobsy calling him smart, but Coop wasn't showing it. Real geniuses didn't guess; they proved. "Let me ask you a question now, since you want to tell me about myself. You tell me about yourself. How did you learn to disable alarm systems? How do you know how to form nonprofits? Why doesn't your brother like you? And why is the phrase 'a dollar and a dream' so important to him?"

Coop reeled back in his seat like he'd been shot, and Charly knew her question about Mēkel had hurt him. He ran his palms over his face in frustration, then looked out the front window. "I taught myself how to disable alarms." He shook his head. "Most number sequences have patterns, but not all. And patterns can usually be broken down into systems. Systems can be reconfigured once you learn them. Something like that. It's hard for me to explain. I don't do textbook talk." He glanced at her. "I just kind of know this stuff. It's always been natural. And any good attorney can tell you how to form a nonprofit, Charly."

Charly pressed her lips together and crossed her arms. "And Mēkel?"

Coop put his face in his palms again, then ran them over his head. "He thinks I abandoned them. And I did." He sat back and quieted for a minute. He banged the steering wheel. "Okay. Here it is. My moms was traveling around, trying to get the lowdown on Bobsy's condition. She was trying to see if some doctor in some other country or hospital had some way of fixing it. I was on babysitting patrol." He looked at Charly intensely, and his eyes were apologetic. "I didn't know what to do, Charly. We were pretty broke back then, and there was no money in the house. My mom had left some behind, and I'd spent it on food, etc., and the last thing I wanted to do was worry her while she was searching for help. And that day, Bobsy ran out of meds. So I did what I knew how to do—well, what the hood we came from expected boys like me to do. I went out in the street to earn it the street way, and I got popped." He threw up his hands. "I was borderline nerd, so I didn't know what I was doing. I got locked up, and Social Services came and took Mēkel and Bobsy because they were so young."

"Oh, no," Charly said, reaching over and touching his arm.

Coop nodded. "Another long story short: Because of how the system is structured, the courts found my mom incompetent of being a mother for months, because she'd left Mēkel and Bobsy with me, and Mēkel was sent one place and, somehow, Bobsy ended up with Lex's family. Lex's family has always helped people. Eventually, Mēkel wound up with Lex and 'em too." He threw her a sideways look. "And before you ask, they helped Faizon too. Lex's pops was like Faizon's mentor—big brother, I think they call it. That's why I said Faizon knew better than to call the cops on me if the alarm went off—we're all like family, which is why he helped us when our house burned down. He did it to help us and to give Lex a break from having to do all the good deeds." He paused, then breathed deeply. "You meant to say, 'stuck between a dollar and a dream.' That was our old saying, Mēkel used to always say that, meaning he was stuck between his dreams and our poorness. He also told Bobsy he felt like he was stuck between foster care and his family. My mom used to say it because we were stuck between finding a cure for Bobsy and the dream of her being cured." He stopped talking, then looked at Charly, and seemed to be waiting for a reaction. "Okay, so can we go pick up this yucky vegan food now?"

Charly laughed, taken off guard. "Vegan food?"

"Yes, our ammunition. Approach Lex with some vegan food, and he can never say no. Especially if it's good. What did you think I was going to get, real weapons?" Coop asked.

Charly looked at her watch and cringed. 2:55 PM. "Coop, can we go get some other kind of food?"

Coop shook his head. "Lex isn't crazy about all the vegan restaurants, so this one is the best bet. Why, what kind of food did you have in mind?"

Charly held her breath and prayed silently. "I was thinking the kind of food Mēkel likes. His concert starts at eight, and I promised Bobsy I'd find him. You were wrong, Coop. I'm not doing this for money or just a new show—not anymore." She shook her head. "I want to help girls like me, girls who come from the 'wrong side' of the street," she said, making quote marks in the air. "And my latest mission is to convince the guys to offer programs for them too. If not for me, just consider it for Bobsy, Coop. She wants it too. So essentially, me and Bobsy are stuck between a dollar and a dream." Her phone vibrated, showing she had a text message from Liam.

LIAM: Lex is here. Was at his old training camp
across town, not in Cali. His fight is tomorrow, not in
a couple days!!!

Coop put the car in D, then clicked on the signal light
and eased into traffic. "All right. You got my attention,
Charly. Because of Bobsy and this 'dollar and a dream'
thing, I'm listening. But you better convince me before
we get to this spot that sells food that Mēkel likes or else
I'm turning around."

Charly shrugged. Lola had been wrong about interviews always coming after boxing matches. "Well, let me
get to convincing because there's no turning around to
get to Lex. Not unless you plan on taking me back to
Vegas."

18

Charly slipped an orange and white floral dress over her shoulders, then looked around the room as if extra clothing and options would appear. She'd contemplated what she should wear ever since Coop had agreed to take her to Mēkel's concert and she'd had her people— i.e. the network—contact Mēkel's people—i.e. Mēkel's publicist and the management at the Staples Center, where he was performing. She growled in frustration. Her choices were minimal. Coop had gotten all of her luggage except for the two bags she needed most, leaving her almost outfit-less and, she discovered, devoid of proper shoes. She could wear either the sneakers that Lex had given her, which were now unacceptable and dirty, or her trusty combat boots with the bright red laces.

"Yo, Charly, the TV said it's going to rain tonight and it may get cooler. You almost ready?" Coop asked from outside the bedroom door.

Charly blinked slowly, thinking of what ready meant and what it would mean later when her dad, Mr. Day, and every other adult whom she had to answer to found out she'd had a convicted criminal book her a hotel room. She knew they wouldn't care that she hadn't planned on booking it, but had to after the Faizon incident, and that she'd only have it for less than twenty-four hours, until she could fly out to Las Vegas.

"One sec," she said, making her way over to an open suitcase and pulling out a pair of purple tights and a studded denim jacket with skull and crossbones on the sleeve. "At least it's outlined in red, so it'll kinda match," she told herself, then slipped into the hosiery.

Coop knocked on the door just as Charly was putting on her boots. "Can I come in? You dressed?"

"Come on, Coop," she said, lacing the boots halfway up. She smiled when he entered. "Coop, you clean up well. You don't look so scary now. What's up?"

He ran his hand over his freshly brushed hair, then popped the collar on his shirt. "It's amazing how fast you can pick out an outfit. Good thing we're right by a shopping center. Good looking on the clothes, Charly. I put all my money into helping the boys out, so I don't spend on myself." He winked. "I was coming in here to see if you need me to carry anything and to let you know I'll go to the concert with you, but I don't want to see Mékel. I never do anyway."

Charly crinkled her brows. "What does that mean? You never see him? How?"

Coop beamed. "Well, I go to all his shows if he's performing close to me, but he doesn't know it. We fight, but I'm proud of him. . . ." He looked away, and it was obvious that his thoughts were taking over. "So, do you want me to carry anything?" he asked.

Charly shook her head no, but her mind was saying *yes*! Coop's keeping up with Mēkel was a positive clue she needed because it told her that there was still some sort of love between the brothers, even if it did seem one-sided. "I'm good until the morning. The network just emailed me my flight confirmation. I'm flying out on the first flight to Las Vegas in the morning. I have to get to Lex before his fight."

Coop nodded. "That's right. He fights tomorrow."

Charly nodded with him. "Yes, so that means I'll be pressed for time. I heard his dad won't let him see anyone before the matches, and that includes me. So I have to catch him at the casino." She looked at her watch. "And I have to catch Mēkel before his show, which means we have to be out. Like right now."

Charly's heart stopped, and her breath caught in her throat. Mēkel stood in front of her, eyeing her with bright eyes and a pleasant smile. He raked his gaze up and down her frame, taking her in. He nodded, then took a long sip from a coffee cup and tossed back his head, gargling. He swallowed, then looked at her. "Tea with honey. It helps my voice," he explained. "So, what are you doing here besides coming to try to talk me back into collaborating on the project or making up with Lex, which is pretty much the same thing?" he asked, arming Charly with helpful knowledge. "I hope you came here for something else. The concert maybe? Because that's all you're getting—the something else." His words were final.

Charly slunk down in the chair behind her and put her face in her hands. She'd traveled to Cali to try to find Mēkel, had talked Coop into having a real sit-down with him instead of a clash of egos, and had put her career and freedom on the line. They would both be in trouble if she didn't get Mēkel to agree to the show and get her behind out of Cali. Now that she was in his dressing room, close enough to smell him, she couldn't find the words to convince him, words she so desperately needed, especially since she'd realized he—and not he and Lex—was the key to the project's success. She gulped back a burning in her chest that signaled tears were in her immediate future. Helplessness was rolling in quickly. Suddenly, she felt as if she couldn't breathe. She'd been in this place before, a situation where someone else—her mother—had been smothering her dream, and she didn't like it. She wasn't going to let Mēkel steal from her too. She just wouldn't give up that easy. She stood. "I'm going to watch the show from my seat," she said. "But before I leave, I want you to know I am here for something else, and I need to ask you a question."

Mēkel straightened the tongue on his white sneakers, which matched his all-white outfit. He looked at her. "So, shoot. What's the question?"

A knock on the dressing room door announced a visitor, interrupting their conversation. A head popped in, and all Charly could see was the back of a baseball cap on a man's head. "Mēkel, you're on in three. Ready?" he asked, then followed Mēkel's eyes to Charly. The man smiled. "Ah, there you are. It's nice to see you again, Charly. Hold up your pass for me." It was Butter Pecan, the same man who'd been protecting Mēkel in the sneaker store in New York. He put a walkie-talkie to his mouth after Charly held up the pass she'd been given by the Staples Center. "I'm going to need an all-access stage pass for Charly from *The Extreme Dream Team*. And set her up stage left," he said to whoever was on the receiving end of his communication. The walkie-talkie crackled, and a voice said something Charly couldn't make out. Butter Pecan turned to her again, pointing toward her chest. "The pass you have now won't allow you on stage or to some other areas back here in backstage, so we have to switch it out. How many pluses do you have?" he asked. Charly held up one finger, then put it down. She remembered what Coop had said; he didn't want Mēkel to know he was there. "None?" Butter Pecan asked, then nodded when she confirmed she was alone. "Good. Good. I hope you don't mind doing a photo shoot immediately after the show, but you and Mēkel need a public appearance to kill the YouTube and other viral controversy." He raised his brows. "Per the network, the record company, and the lawyers." He shot Mēkel a look. "Cool?" he asked only Charly, telling her Mēkel didn't have as much control as he thought he had, at least not over his career.

Charly shrugged. "Well, I don't know. That depends on Mēkel. My career is pretty much a wrap because of him, so I have nothing to lose, but apparently . . ." She looked at Mēkel. "You have a lot to lose." She looked back at Butter Pecan. "I'll be more than happy to be shot with Mēkel—on stage. I want a guest appearance, and he has to accompany me to Las Vegas to see Bobsy. First thing in the morning."

Butter Pecan waited patiently, looking from Mēkel to Charly. Mēkel huffed, but Charly didn't care. "That's dirty, Charly. Okay, back to what you were saying earlier. What's your question? Hurry up, I only have like ten seconds."

Charly smiled. "Have you ever been stuck between a dollar and a dream? Wait. Don't answer that—just think about it while you perform. Oh, and another thing, I'm not here for the concert. I'm here for Bobsy, and other girls. All girls . . . girls like us who need guys like you to help us." She walked over to him, then kissed him on his cheek. "I'll meet you on stage. It's all under your control now."

Charly stood stage left next to Butter Pecan. She peeked out into the audience every so often. The Staples Center was huge and dark and crowded, and for the life of her, she couldn't spot Coop. She knew he was there though, somewhere in the first row. Despite his protests about being seen, his seating was unavoidable thanks to the arrangement her people had made with management. Mēkel hit a high note, pulling her attention back to the stage, and like just about every girl in the audience who screamed, Charly felt him. It was as if he were serenading her and her alone. His voice was that melodic. His words came across that genuine. She could tell he was feeling every lyric he sang. The live band he had accompanying him switched songs, moving into a more hypnotic, up-tempo beat. Her boots tapped in rhythm to it on the floor, and her head bobbed like Mēkel's.

"Whew! It's hot up here. Are you hot out there?" he asked the audience, who answered back. "You sure?" he asked again. " 'Cause if you're not, then I'm not doing my job! Ladies, are you sure I'm doing my job? You need me to get hotter for ya?" He held the mic toward the audience, then smiled when the females in the audience yelled out yes and screamed. Mēkel held his hand in the air, then pushed it palm-down toward the ground, telling the band to lower the volume. "Okay. Okay. I'm going to make it a little hotter out here, but first, I need some assistance in getting this sweat off of me," he teased, making the girls scream. He shot Charly a look. "But this time I'm going to do it a little different. I need professional assistance. . . ."

Charly shook her head, then turned to Butter Pecan, who stood by. "No, he isn't. I know he is not calling me out to wipe his sweat off him."

Butter Pecan laughed, then handed Charly a white towel. "You two did it, now you two fix it."

Mēkel stopped, and turned. He stared at her now, then held the mic close to his mouth. "Yes, professional assistance. Someone who can *extremely* make me over. Ya know, like that show many of you girls love to watch, *The Extreme Dream Team*? Charly. Charly St. James, come on out and wipe this sweat off my brow. It's the least you can do to make up for assaulting me when I was saving you."

Charly put on her best face and walked out, smiling and waving. She'd been here before, and now she wasn't nervous. She walked straight to Mēkel and gave him a tight embrace, then whispered between clenched teeth almost the exact words he'd said to her at RiRi's concert. "This charade isn't for you. It's for the fans, Bobsy, and more importantly, all girls who are hurting. If you can be professional enough, do us all a favor and play along." She let him go, then swallowed her pride and patted his forehead with the towel. She reached out her hand for his mic, then turned to the audience. "Thank you all for watching the show, and please know that me and the entire crew of *The Extreme Dream Team* love you very much. It's because of you all that I'm no longer stuck between a dollar and a dream." She clapped with the audience, who clapped and cheered with her. "And it's because of Mēkel," she began, then cupped one hand around her mouth and pretended to whisper into the microphone, "and two other great guys whose names I don't have to mention—hint, hint, Lex and Faizon—that *The Extreme Dream Team* gets to help with a fabulous retreat for girls in Las Vegas. You all give it up for them. Love you again, and remember to tune in!" She handed the microphone back to Mēkel, then reached up to hug him again. She whispered in his ear, "I was stuck between making the project happen so I can get a spinoff show and my dream of helping girls like me. But you know what, Mēkel? I'm not stuck anymore." She looked at him with pain filled eyes. "I'll take helping girls who have problems like I had over a spinoff any day. Don't you remember what it's like to struggle and hurt and feel like there's no one to help?" she said, then walked off with a pasted-on phony smile.

Butter Pecan nodded his admiration for her as she

made it to stage left. His mouth formed to say something, but he didn't speak. His eyes left her and widened.

Charly turned to see what has captivated him, and came face to face with a sweaty Mēkel. "What—?"

"I remember," was all he said, cutting her off. Then he grabbed her and kissed her.

19

Charly rushed. She hopped on one foot, pulling her slingback strap over her heel as she made it to Lex's dressing room. Her heart was pounding like never before, and she began to question ever dealing with the opposite sex again. She was sure that since encountering the guys and their project, her pulse had never raced so quickly. Ever since she and Mēkel had clashed in the sneaker store, her emotions had been on a roller coaster. She was angry one minute and anxious the next, and she was getting tired of it.

"What took you so long?" Bobsy asked, leaning against the wall next to Lex's dressing room door.

Charly smiled. Bobsy was wearing a dress and makeup, and didn't look a thing like a boy anymore. "You look good, Bobsy. I'm glad the hospital released you." She shook her head. "Don't ask me why, but I talked to Faizon, or whatever he's calling himself until he finishes filming."

"Steel," Bobsy said.

"What?" Charly asked.

"Steel. That's his character name. Anyway, you're late, but right on time. There's a huge fight going on in there." She pointed to Lex's dressing room. "Did you know Coop was coming?"

Now Charly paused. She had had no idea Coop was going to show, and hadn't seen him after he'd dropped her off at her hotel room. "They're fighting?"

Bobsy shook her head. "Figure of speech. But they're working things out. At least they were before they made me leave."

Charly nodded, approaching the door. "Okay, I'm on it," she said, putting her palms against the door, getting ready to push it open.

"Don't!" Bobsy said. "Don't go in there."

The door swung open, making Charly lose her balance. She tumbled forward, and fell into Mēkel's chest. He grabbed her. "Hey! You okay?" he asked. His tone was smooth and calm. "Future wifey." He laughed, and a deeper, raspier voice laughed with him.

Charly looked behind Mēkel and saw Coop. She smiled, then looked up into Mēkel's eyes, and was met with warmth. "I don't know about all of that. Just because we kissed . . ." She bit her lip, flirting, then stood up straight. "I'm glad to see you all worked it out. I'll be right back. I'm going to see Lex."

"No!" Mēkel and Coop said in unison. Their tones were serious. "Don't do that! He's getting in fight mode and needs a minute."

Charly shrugged, then rolled her eyes. She'd come too

far and risked too much to wait. "Whatever," she said, then walked around them. She heard footsteps following behind her, and knew it was them trying to stop her. Lex's arm movements could be heard in the air, swishing.

"Charly," Mēkel's voice called from behind her in a loud whisper as she turned the corner and spotted Lex shadow boxing.

She picked up speed, wanting to get to Lex before Mēkel and Coop caught up to her. He was only a couple of feet away, she noted. She lengthened her steps, then reached out to touch his shoulder. "Hey—" she began, then stopped. Her face cracked. The room darkened. Her body was airborne, moving upward, then backward, and then lowering to the ground. *What's happening?* She wondered, then heard a faint voice. *They say a person's hearing is the last to go, so I can't be dead. Yet.*

"Oh, ish!" Lex's voice yelled. "I didn't mean to knock her out. I was just warming up . . . and something touched me. Made me jump. React."

Something warm was touching her hand, and the wind had a minty smell. Charly inhaled, enjoying the cool sensation and wishing the air always smelled so sweet. She smiled, relaxed, then tensed. She flailed her arms. Someone was trying to drown her in ice water, she was sure.

"She's up. She's up. Charly, are you okay? Can you hear me?" a beautiful, raspy voice asked.

Mēkel?

"Charly, love. Squeeze my hand if you hear me. C'mon, love. You're scaring me."

Liam. Oh my Liam. Charly smiled. She could never

hear his accent enough, and loved the way he spoke her name. She opened her eyes, and almost jumped out of her skin. There in front of her, only inches away from her face, were the two finest dudes she'd ever met. Mēkel, whose breath was minty, and Liam, whose hand was warm, were both kneeling beside her. "What happened?" she asked, trying to sit up. "Why am I on the floor?"

"Well," Lex said, suddenly standing over her. He was scratching his head and pacing. "I kinda knocked you out." His expression said he was sorry. "You can't sneak up on people like that, Charly. Mēkel and Coop said they tried to stop you. Bobsy too. Please tell me you're all right. I need to know you're okay before I go out here in this ring and lose. I can't win with you back here hurt, and if the press finds out about this—skip the press, if the boxing commission or the police find this out—I won't be able to fight anymore."

Charly grabbed onto Mēkel and Liam, and pulled herself up into a sitting position. She may've just been knocked out, but she wasn't dazed or confused about what she wanted. "Well, Lex. I'll tell you what. If you all agree to get this project rolling, to get this retreat and other retreats for all ill girls—physically, mentally, emotionally, and economically sick girls—I might recover from you knocking me out." She winked. "And if you go out there, knock out your opponent in less than five rounds, *and* make the project happen—I'll forget this ever happened, and put it in writing too."

Lex bounced up and down in place, warming up. "Bet. I'll knock him out in two rounds . . . but only if you have the dinner with me that you owe me."

Epilogue

Charly put a hand on her hip, then looked at the line of masking tape on the floor. With careful steps and a book on her head, she put one foot in front of the other, scaling it as if it were a tightrope. With precision, she crossed one ankle in front of the other, then twisted around, facing the other way. "Got it?" she asked, rolling her eyes and shaking her head. She couldn't believe she was doing what she was doing, but she was.

Faizon stood next to her, nodding. "Like this?" he asked, just a bit too femininely, then tried to mimic her walk, which was also over the top.

"No, Faizon. No," Bobsy said from the side of the room. "Girls don't prance like that. We walk."

Faizon put his hand on his hip, then wiggled his polished pink nails. "You swish when you walk. What's the difference between prancing and swishing?" he asked, then adjusted his blush-colored blouse.

Loud laughter erupted as Mēkel, Lex, Coop, and Liam entered the theater room.

"Shuddup," Faizon shouted in a high-pitched voice.

"Yo, Fai. I'm out. I can't do this," Coop said, then turned on his heel. "I can't see you like this. I don't care if you did chip in to help pay for our crib when it burned."

Mēkel laughed, holding up a fist to his mouth. "Coop, it's cool. You know Faizon always lives as his character. It's a front though, and you know it. Y'all don't mind, do you, ladies?" Mēkel turned toward the girls in the audience.

"No, they don't mind," Lex said, smiling. "These are theater arts ladies, which is why they're in the theater wing."

"Mmm, I don't know, Lex. Some of us, maybe. But I don't know how long I can watch Faizon make a fool out of us girls. We don't act like he's acting. I may be coming over to the boxing area or learning how to sing soon," the other Charlie said, then smiled. Her baby was in the seat next to her in a car seat. Eden sat next to her, dressed as a character, nodding in agreement too.

Liam walked over to Charly, then put his arm around her. "You know, Charly number two, you can always come over to the other wing and learn construction. I'm quite the teacher," he said, praising himself. "If you don't believe me, ask Whip. He helped me build the stage Faizon's on now."

"Yep. 'Cause Whip's built for more than speed!" Whip shouted from behind.

Charly smiled. She didn't know if Liam had put his

arm around her out of sincerity or competitiveness. He and Mēkel had been in constant competition for her full attention since they had started planning and building the retreat for girls, and she didn't care. She liked the attention, and loved that she didn't have to choose between them. As far as her fans were concerned, she was Liam's. In Mēkel's mind, it was only a matter of time before she became his girlfriend. To Charly, she was just Charly St. James, and she could and would have the best of both worlds. She had *The Extreme Dream Team* and was shooting a pilot series that would help girls from all walks of life from the inside out, and she'd managed to get the guys to help all girls too.

BEWARE OF BOYS

Kelli London

ABOUT THIS GUIDE

The following questions are intended to
enhance your group's reading of
BEWARE OF BOYS.

Discussion Questions

1. Charly literally had boy trouble. Every problem she encountered involved either a guy or someone whom she thought was a guy. Because Charly was the common denominator in each problem, could Charly possibly have been the real problem?

2. As a reality television star, Charly has received much, and therefore was driven to give much, even if it meant sacrificing her dream of getting another reality show. Have you ever wanted to help a person or cause so badly that you'd sacrifice your dreams? Discuss.

3. Charly will do just about anything to get what she wants, including "bending" the truth, hiding things from the adults in her life, and twisting someone's arm (i.e. holding something against someone to make them deliver). Though we know right from wrong, were her actions justifiable? Is there ever a reason to use bad to make good things happen?

4. Charly was surrounded by some of the hottest guys on the planet, and was tempted by their looks and star power. However, she kept her eyes on the bigger picture—getting a place of refuge for girls—

and that required strength. Do you think you could've done the same?

5. In *Beware of Boys*, we met Charlie, a young teenage mother, who was enrolled in community college. It was clear her life was a struggle, yet she still pursued her education. Other than educational and financial setbacks, what do you think are some other problems that come with teenage pregnancy and parenting?

6. Charlie, the young teenage mother, implied a sort of prejudice against certain communities being broadcasted by saying reality shows don't showcase "real" everyday people or "at risk" communities, and Charly readily agreed. Do you think their assessment is true? Do you see all communities showcased on your television screen? If not, why?

7. Charly, though a good girl, consorted with ex-criminals to help her achieve her dream, and put herself at risk to get what she wanted. Do you think Charly was too trusting when she was alone with Coop? Was she herself a criminal by "allowing" him to break into Faizon's house or "borrowing" Faizon's car?

8. "Disease \diz-'ēz\ (adjective)
An impairment of the normal state of the living animal or plant body or one of its parts that interrupts or modifies the performance of the vital

functions, is typically manifested by distinguishing signs and symptoms, and is a response to environmental factors (as malnutrition, industrial hazards, or climate), to specific infective agents (as worms, bacteria, or viruses), to inherent defects of the organism (as genetic anomalies), or to combinations of these factors."—Merriam Webster Dictionary

Mēkel, Faizon, and Lex viewed illness according to what they'd been exposed to (diagnosed medical issues), and Charly believed illness to include mental, emotional, and physical suffering, such as being down and out, a victim of an unstable home, low self-esteem, etc. What's your take? Should all the above be considered because some other "unseen" ailments cause *dis*ease in a person?

Meet Charly for the first time in . . .

Charly's Epic Fiascos.

Available wherever books are sold!

This is going to be easy. Simple. "Turn. Turn. Turn!" Charly said, grabbing her little sister, Stormy, by the forearm. She shoved her hip into Stormy's side, forcing her thin frame to round the corner of the schoolyard. Her feet quickened with each step. They were almost home-free.

"Ouch!" Stormy hissed, cradling her torn backpack to her bosom like an infant in an attempt to prevent her books from falling onto the cracked sidewalk. "All this for Mason? Serious? Let go of my arm, Charly. Let me go. If I had known we'd be up here mixed up in drama, I wouldn't have come to meet you. I need to get home and study."

Charly rolled her eyes. Being at home is exactly where her sister needed to be. She hadn't asked Stormy to meet her. In fact, she remembered telling her not to come. She'd had beef with one of the cliques over nothing—not him, as Stormy thought. Nothing, meaning the girls were hating on Charly for being her fabulous self and for being Mason's girl. She held two spots they all seemed to want but couldn't have. She was the It Girl who'd snagged the hottest boy that had ever graced her town. "Go home, Stormy," she said, semi-pushing her sister ahead.

"Do it again and I'm going to—" Stormy began.

"You're going to go home. That's all you're going to do," Charly said matter-of-factly, then began looking around. She was searching for Lola, her best friend. If she had to act a fool, she'd prefer to show out with Lola around, not Stormy. She had to protect her younger sister, not Lola. Lola was a force to be reckoned with and she wasn't afraid of anyone or anything.

A crowd came her and Stormy's way, swarming around them as the students made their way down the block. A shoulder bumped into Charly, pushing her harder than it should have. Charly squared her feet, not allowing herself to fall. Quickly, she scanned the group, but was unable to tell who the culprit was. "If you're bad enough to bump into me while you're in a group, be bad enough to do it solo. Step up," Charly dared whoever.

Stormy pulled her as some members of the crowd turned toward them. "Come on, Charly. Not today," Stormy begged. "Remember the school said if you have one more incident you'd get suspended."

Charly grabbed Stormy's arm again, preparing to jump in front of her in case the person who pushed her stepped forward.

"Hey, baby," Mason called, pushing through the crowd. "Everything good?" he asked, making his way to her and

Stormy. "Or do we gotta be about it?" he asked, then threw a nasty look over his shoulder to the group. " 'Cause I know they don't want that." His statement was a threat, and everyone knew it. Just as Charly was protective over her sister, Mason was protective over her. His lips met her cheek before she could answer him.

"We're fine, Mason," Stormy offered.

Mason nodded. "Better be. They're just mad 'cause they're not you. But you know that. Right?"

Charly smiled. Yes, she knew.

"Good. Listen, I need to run back into the school for a minute," he said, reaching down for her book bag.

Charly hiked it up on her shoulder. "You can go ahead. We're good. I promise."

He stood and watched the crowd disperse and start to thin before he spoke. "All right. I'll catch up to you two in a few." He disappeared into the crowd of students still on school grounds.

"So really, Charly? You were going to fight whoever over him?" Stormy asked again.

Charly ignored the question as she focused on parting the crowd. They needed to get down the block.

"Hey, Charly! Call me later. There's something I want to talk to you about," a girl shouted from across the street.

Charly looked over and nodded. She couldn't have remembered the girl's name if she'd wanted to, let alone her number. Obviously the girl knew her though, but who didn't?

"Catch up with me tomorrow," she answered, then released her grip on Stormy and sucked her teeth at her sister's questioning. Stormy had no idea. Mason was the new guy around and the guy of her dreams. They'd been dating, but she couldn't let him know just how much he had her because then she'd be like every other girl in their town. And she refused to be like the others, acting crazy over a guy.

"Mason, Charly? That's what this is all about?" Stormy asked again.

"Shh," Charly said, shushing her sister. "What did I tell you about that? Stop saying his name, Stormy."

Stormy shook her head and her eyes rolled back in her head. "Serious? What, calling his name is like calling Bloody Mary or something? I *so* thought that Bloody Mary thing only worked with Bloody Mary's name and Brigette's generation. Who believes in such stuff, Charly? You can call anyone's name as many times as you like."

Charly got tense with the mention of their mother. Brigette refused to be called anything besides her given name, and Mom, Mommy, and Mother were definitely out of the question. That she'd made clear. On top of that, she insisted her name be pronounced the correct *French* way, Bri-jeet, not Bridge-jit.

"Please don't bring her up. My afternoon is already hectic enough. I don't wanna have to deal with Brigette until I have to," Charly said, her quick steps forcing rocks to spit from the backs of her shoes. "Just c'mon. And, like you, I need to get my homework done before I go to work. Mr. Miller said if my math assignment is late one more time, he'll fail me. And I can't have that. Not right before we go on break for a week. And I don't want to do any sort of schoolwork while we're out. Oh!" She froze.

A dog ran toward them at top speed from between two bushes, then was snatched back by the chain leash around its neck. It yelped, then wagged its tail, barking. Charly, a little nervous, managed strength and pushed Stormy out of harm's way. Looking into the dog's eyes, she was almost afraid to move. She'd distrusted dogs since she was five, when her mother had convinced her they were all vicious, and now her feelings for them bordered on love/hate. She'd loved them once, and now hated that they made her uncomfortable, but was now determined to get over her fear. A pet salon near her home was hiring, and, whether she liked dogs or not, she needed more money for her new phone and other things.

The wind blew back Charly's hair, exposing the forehead that she disliked so much. Unlike Stormy, she hadn't inherited her mother's, which meant on a breezy day like today, her forehead looked like a miniature sun, a globe as her mother had called it when she was upset. On her mom's really peeved days, which were often, she'd refer to Charly as Headquarters. Charly smoothed her hairdo in place, not knowing what else to do.

Stormy grabbed her arm. "C'mon, Charly. We go through this at least twice a week. You know Keebler's not going to bite you, just like you know he can't break that chain." She shrugged. "I don't know why you're so scared. You used to have a dog, remember? Marlow . . . I think that's the name on the picture. It's in Brigette's photo album."

Charly picked up speed. Her red bootlaces blew in the wind, clashing against the chocolate of her combats. Yes, she'd had a dog named Marlow for a day, then had come home and found Marlow was gone. Charly had never forgotten about her, but, still, she'd believed her mother then, and now couldn't shake the uneasiness when one approached. Especially Keebler. He'd tried to attack her when he was younger, and she still feared him. So what if he'd gotten old? Teeth were still teeth, and dogs' fangs were sharp. "How do you know he won't bite, Stormy? You say that about every dog."

Stormy laughed, jogging behind her. "Well, Charly. Keebler's older than dirt, he doesn't have teeth, and that chain is made for big dogs, I'm thinking over a hundred pounds. Keebler's twenty, soaking wet. What, you think he's going to gnaw you to death?"

Charly had to laugh. She'd forgotten Keebler was minus teeth. "Okay. Maybe you're right. We only have two more blocks," she said, slowing her walk. Her pulse began to settle when she caught sight of the green street sign in the distance, and knew she'd soon be closer to home than barking Keebler. "Only two more and you can get to your precious studying, nerd," she teased Stormy, who laughed. They both knew how proud Charly was of Stormy's intelligence. Stormy didn't hit the books because she needed to; she had to, it was her addiction. "And I can knock out this assignment," she added.

"Yo, Chi-town Charly! Hold up!" Mason called, his footsteps growing louder with each pound on the concrete.

Charly picked up her pace. She wanted to stop but she couldn't. Boyfriend or not, he had to chase her. That's what kept guys interested. Stormy halted in her tracks, kicked out her leg, and refused to let Charly pass. "What's going on now? Why are you ignoring Mason? Oops, I said his name again." Stormy sighed, pushing up her glasses on her nose.

Charly rolled her eyes. "I'm not really ignoring Mason, Stormy. Watch and learn—I'm just keeping him interested," she said, failing to tell her sister that she was trying to come up with an explanation for disappearing the weekend before. She'd told him she was going to visit her family in New York, and now she just needed to come up with the details. Her chest rose, then fell, letting out her breath in a heavy gasp. What she'd hoped to be a cleansing exhale sputtered out in frustration. "He may be a New Yorker, but we're from the South Side of Chicago. I got to keep the upper hand." She repeated the mantra she used whenever she had to face a problem, but it was no use. The truth was, yes, they had been born on the South Side of Chicago, but now they lived almost seventy miles away from their birthplace in an old people's town. She couldn't wait to leave.

Mason's hand was on her shoulder before Charly knew it. She froze. Turning around was not just an option; she had to. She knew that he knew that she'd heard him now. Summoning her inner actress, she became the character she played for him. Charly switched gears from teenage girl to potential and future Oscar nominee. She erased the glee of him chasing her down from her face and became who and what he knew her to be. Cool, calm, self-assured Charly—the girl who seemed to have it all. Seemed being the operative word since she lacked teen essentials like the Android phone she was saving for and a computer.

"Hey! I said hold up. Guess you didn't hear me. Right?" His voice was rugged and his words seemed final, as if he had nothing else to say. His tone spoke for him. It was sharp and clipped, yet something about it was smooth. Just hearing him speak made her feel good.

She smiled when she turned and faced him. "Hi, Mason. I'm sorry. There's so much wind blowing that I couldn't hear you."

Mason smiled back and did that thing with his eyebrows that made her melt every time. He didn't really raise or wiggle them, but they moved slightly and caused his eyes to light. "Yeah. So . . ." he began, then quieted, throwing Stormy a *please?* look.

"Okay. Okay. Personal space. I get it," Stormy said, then began to walk ahead of them. "You high schoolers are sickening."

Mason smiled at Stormy's back, and Charly grimaced behind it. She hadn't asked Stormy to give her and Mason alone time, and wished that her sister hadn't. The last thing she wanted was to be alone with Mason because every time she was, her lies piled. They'd stacked so high that now she couldn't see past them, and had no idea how to get around or through them.

"So, I've been trying to catch up with you to see how New York was last weekend when you went to visit your pops. You did fly out for the weekend, right?" he asked, his eyes piercing hers like he knew she hadn't gone.

She scrunched her brows together. It was time to flesh out her partial untruths. She thought of her semi-truths that way because to her they were. She'd done and been and imagined it all in her head, so, in a way, her not-so-trues were kind-of-trues.

"Uh, yeah." *Here comes the hook*, she thought while she felt the fattening lie forming on the back of her tongue, pushing its way out her mouth. "Right. But it was no biggie. I wasn't even there a whole two days. I was in and out of Newark before I knew it. I visited my dad and my aunt. She works for a television station— where they film reality shows. One day I'm going to be on one. That's the plan—to become a star."

"Newark? That's Jersey. I thought you said you were flying into Queens." He looked at her, pressing his lips together. He'd totally ignored her star statement.

"Queens? Did I say Queens?" *Dang it*. She shrugged, trying to think of a cover.

"Yep. You said your pops was picking you up at La-Guardia airport. That's in Queens. Guess Newark was cheaper, huh?" He waved his hand at her. "Same difference. Me and my fam do it too. Sometimes it pays to fly into Jersey instead. It's about the same distance when you consider traffic time instead of miles."

Charly nodded, pleased that Mason's travel knowledge had saved her. "Yeah. I know that's right. And I got there when traffic was mad hectic too. I'm talking back to back, bumper to bumper. But it was cool though. Manhattan's always cool, Brooklyn too," she lied about both. She'd never been to Manhattan and she was only five when she'd visited Brooklyn. But she'd gone to places like Central Park and Times Square all the time in her mind, and a mental trip to the Big Apple had to count for something.

"Brooklyn, yeah, it's cool. Matter of fact, I miss home so much, I just got a puppy and named her Brooklyn." He smiled.

Charly raised her brows. "Really? That's hot. I just love dogs. In fact, I just applied for a gig working at the pet salon." Another partial lie. She had planned on applying, she just hadn't had time yet.

Nodding in appreciation, his smile grew. "That's good, Charly. And it couldn't have come at a better time." He took her book bag from her, then slung it over his shoulder. "Dang. This is heavy. What'chu got in it?"

"Math," Charly said. "I got to ace this assignment, so I brought home my book and every book the library would let me check out to make sure I get it right. Because I go to New York so much, I kind of fell behind on the formulas," she added. She couldn't have him think her anything less than a genius.

Mason nodded. "Good thinking. Knock it out from all angles. Math is the universal language. Did you know that?" he asked, but didn't give her time to answer. "Let's walk," he said, clearly not letting up. "It must be nice to have your pops send for you a couple times a month. So what'd you do all weekend? Party?"

She kicked pebbles out of her way, wishing they were

her lies. She hadn't seen her father since she was five, and it was something that was hard for her to admit, especially since Stormy's dad was still on the scene for birthdays and holidays. The truth was she had no idea where her father was, so she imagined him still living in New York, where she'd last seen him.

"So did you party?" Mason repeated.

Me, party? Yeah, right! My mom partied while I worked a double shift to save for a new phone. Then I sat holed up in the house on some fake punishment. "Yeah, actually I did. Nothing big though. It was a get-together for my aunt. You know, the one I told you about who's a big shot at the network. Well, she just got promoted, and now she's an even bigger big shot. She's got New York on lock."

Mason nodded, then slowed his pace as Charly's house came into view. "That's cool, Charly. Real cool. It's nice to finally have a friend I can chop it up with. Ya know, another city person who can relate. Somebody who gets where I'm from. Not too many people around here can keep up with my Brooklyn pace," he said, referring to the almost-dead town they lived in. Their tiny city was okay for older people, but teens had it bad. They lived in a nine-mile-square radius with only about twenty-five thousand other people. There was only one public high school and one emergency room, which equated to too small and everybody knowing everyone else and their business. Nothing was sacred in Belvidere, Illinois.

Charly took her book bag from Mason. "Trust me, I know. They can't keep up with my Chi-Town pace either. I'm getting out of here ASAP."

He walked her to her door. "Speaking of ASAP. You still gonna be able to come through with helping me with my English paper this week? I have to hand it in right after break, so I'd really like to get it finished as soon as possible. Don't wanna be off from school for a week and have to work." He shrugged. "But I know you're pressed with school and getting an A on the math assignment. Plus, with flying back and forth to New York to check your pops, and trying to work at the pet salon, I know you're busy. But I really need you, Charly," he paused, throwing her a sexy grin that made her insides melt. "I don't even know what a thesis statement is, let alone where one goes in an essay."

Charly smiled, then purposefully bit her tongue to prevent herself from lying again. She'd forgotten when Mason's paper was due. An essay she would be no better at writing than he would. She sucked in English, but couldn't pass up the opportunity to be close to him. "I gotta work tonight and pretty much all week," she said. She was finally kinda sorta truthful. She did have to work. Now that she was sixteen, and had snatched up a job at a local greasy spoon—and, hopefully, the pet salon she'd told him she had applied at—it was up to her to make sure that the electric and cable bills were paid, plus she had to pay for her own clothing. "We've been *very* busy at work, for some reason."

"Okay." Mason grimaced, then looked past her, apparently deep in thought. He rubbed his chin. "I don't know what I'm going to do now. I gotta pass this class. . . ."

Charly pressed her lips together. She couldn't let him down. It was because of her that he'd waited so long to tackle the paper. She'd told him not to worry, that she had him, that she was something like an A or B English student. Now, it'd seem as if her word was no good, and she couldn't have that.

"Kill the worry, Mason. I'll work it out."